Wolcum Yole

Susan Alexander

MINERVA

SUSAN ALEXANDER

Copyright 2014 by Susan Alexander

All rights reserved.

All characters in this publication are fictional.
Any resemblance to persons living or dead is purely coincidental.

Also by the author

The Snowdrop Mysteries:
The Ainswick Orange
The Snowdrop Crusade
A Remittance Man
The Heracles Project
St Margaret's
Beaumatin's Blonde
Hereford Crescent

A Woman's Book of Rules

Illustrations of G. elwesii Wolcum Yole
by Freda Cox

WOLCUM YOLE

To Gudrun and Claude

and

Kerry and Chris

For good crémant enjoyed in even better company

Susan Alexander

Wolcum Yole

Wolcum Yole

Wolcum be thou hevenè king. Wolcum Yole!
Wolcum, born in one morning. Wolcum for whom we sall sing.

Wolcum be ye Stevene and Jon. Wolcum Innocentes everyone.
Wolcum, Thomas marter one. Wolcum, be ye, Good Newe Yere.
Wolcum, seintes lefe and dere, Wolcum Yole! Wolcum!

Candelmesse, Quene of bliss. Wolcum bothe to more and lesse.

Wolcum be ye that are here. Wolcum Yole!
Wolcum alle and make good cheer. Wolcum alle another yere.
Wolcum Yole! Wolcum!

Anonymous. 14th century.

"Wolcom Yole," meaning Welcome Yule or Welcome Christmas, is a fourteenth century poem by an anonymous author written in Middle English.

Used by Benjamin Britten (1913.1976) in his choral piece *Ceremony of Carols* op. 28, (1942), the work consists of eleven movements scored for three-part treble chorus, solo voices and harp.

A magical performance of this piece can be found on YouTube at http://youtu.be/pQyunriE1zg

Susan Alexander

Chapter 1

Maggie was pleased with herself for several reasons. First, in her role as Professor Margaret Spence Eliot, Appleton Fellow for Global Issues at Merrion College, Oxford, she had just survived a week of media appearances and interviews to promote the launch of a new book she had written. Called *Fitting In*, it documented the greater success of immigrant families to the UK who adapted to the culture of their new country rather than tried to preserve the customs of their old.

The liberals hated her views, despite her having the research to back them up. Equally as bad, the conservatives assumed her work meant she was also anti-Muslim and anti-immigration. Which she was not and frequently had to set the record straight by launching into lectures on the contributions of Islam to the world as well what immigrants had contributed to Britain.

Her best moment had come when a liberal Talking Head was haranguing her on live television. When he had not paused to draw breath for nearly a minute, she took a copy of her book off his desk, turned her chair so that her back was to him and started leafing through the pages.

"What do you think you're doing?" he had yelled.

"Just checking. As I am certain I never wrote anything like what you're saying. Are you sure this is the book you read?"

A *Guardian* headline the next day trumpeted, "The Burqa Burner Strikes Again." The morning that came out she was meeting with her publisher, Malcolm Fortescue-Smythe.

"Let's hope what they say about there being no such thing as bad publicity is true," he said philosophically. "And certainly all this hoo-ha will be great for when your other book comes out in January."

The book that Maggie was currently promoting was primarily targeted at other scholars, pundits and policy makers. Fortescue-Smythe had thought there could also be popular interest in her work and, consequently, a more "accessible" edition was being launched in a few weeks.

So Maggie was pleased that the launch had gone well. And was equally pleased that it was over.

She was also pleased that Michaelmas term at Oxford had ended and she could spend the next five weeks enjoying being with Thomas, her husband. Since their wedding had only been in May she supposed she could even consider him her new husband. And she was just about home.

Home. Well, Thomas' home. Maggie was not sure she would ever think of it as her home. The tall, green-eyed American with her unruly auburn curls still tended to consider her native Boston as home. And it was not simply a question of geographic location. Thomas was the 28th Baron Raynham and lived on an estate in the Cotswolds. Not large enough to be a stately home, Beaumatin, with its eccentric mix of Elizabethan, Jacobean, Georgian and Victorian Gothic architecture, was still large enough that there were parts Maggie had yet to visit. A servants wing, for instance, that was now unused. And a wine cellar.

Beaumatin was also famous for its gardens and especially for its snowdrops. Maggie liked the gardens. She was less fond of the sheep, which occupied most of the rest of Beaumatin's acres and seemed to take up a lot of Thomas' time.

Wolcum Yole

Maggie drove through Beaumatin's elaborate wrought iron gates and up its tree-lined drive.

"Out of the frying pan, into the fire," she muttered.

If the book launch were the frying pan, the fire was the upcoming wedding of Thomas' daughter Constance. Constance was his youngest child from his first marriage. His wife Harriet had died of cancer five years previously.

Constance was an epidemiologist at the World Health Organisation in Geneva. Her Swedish fiancé, Nils von Fersen, also worked there and the wedding was scheduled for the Saturday before Christmas.

Constance would arrive the week before that to oversee preparations. Nils' family, who would also be staying at Beaumatin, would arrive a few days later. Maggie, whose relationship with Constance was tepid at best, had not been consulted about any of the arrangements.

"You are not a lesser woman", Maggie reminded herself as she pulled up in front of the house. "You will rise to this occasion, be a charming and attentive hostess and make Thomas proud that he married you. Only a lesser woman would want to book the next flight to Ulan Bator."

Maggie descended from the pine green Land Rover, which had been a birthday present from Thomas. Before her feet touched the ground, the front door opened and Thomas came out.

"Welcome home," he said and gave her a hug.

"Thank you. I won't say that was the worst week of my life, but it was certainly one of the more unpleasant."

"I thought you did well. Quite well, in fact. Although I'm not sure many of those interviewers were up to your weight," Thomas said.

Maggie digested this equestrian reference for a moment, then smiled.

As they entered the great hall, with its black and white checkerboard marble floor, oak panelling and ancestral portrait gallery, Maggie heard someone call, "Hi, Maggie."

She looked up. It was Derek Fiske, a garden designer whom she had met at the same time she had met Thomas. He had subsequently become a friend. He was on the landing of the grand staircase and slid down the bannister to greet her.

"Derek, really!"

It was Derek's partner, Damien Hawking, who emerged from the music room. Both men were attractive, in their thirties, and similarly dressed in jeans and chequered shirts.

"Hi, Maggie. We watched you on television. You did good."

"Thank you, Damien."

"Fiske and Hawking are here taking measurements for the decorations for Constance's do," Thomas explained.

"Ornamental grasses?" Maggie teased.

"No," said Damien regretfully.

"But only because he couldn't figure out how to string them with fairy lights," said Derek.

Wolcum Yole

"So we're going to be decking your halls in a more traditional style," Damien continued.

"Boughs of holly, then," Maggie said.

"Fir, actually. And a small forest of pines. And the biggest Christmas tree we can find."

"And fairy lights everywhere," Derek finished.

Maggie noticed Thomas was looking pained.

"It all sounds very Winter Wonderland," she said, trying to avert any "Bah humbugs" from her husband.

"That's what Constance asked for. And designing something like this indoors isn't really that different than designing a garden outdoors. At least that's what Lady Ainswick thought. We were happy she recommended us."

The Ainswicks were old friends of Thomas and also had a famous snowdrop garden at nearby Rochford Manor. It was at a snowdrop study weekend there the previous February which Maggie had improbably attended that she had met the Ainswicks, as well as Derek, Damien and Thomas.

"Well, we have the measurements we need. So we'll be off," said Damien.

"See you next week," said Derek.

The men left.

Thomas looked at Maggie.

"We weren't sure when you'd arrive. I know Mrs Cook has some soup she can fix."

Mrs Cook was the Beaumatin housekeeper and always seemed to have some soup in reserve.

"But I thought you might want to rest first. Lie down for a bit?"

Maggie was about to say she was not particularly tired, when she noticed Thomas' expression. And she had been away for more than a week.

"Lie down for a bit? All right."

Resting could come later.

Chapter 2

The next morning, Maggie woke up in what she liked to think of as "a tangle of Thomas."

"This is nice," she thought.

Thomas also seemed to be awake.

"God, I missed you," he said and kissed her.

"Me too. I…"

"Shh."

Maggie thought about how unlikely it had been that she had ever met Thomas. And how equally unlikely it had been that, when she realised she had become completely besotted with the man, he had seemed to care for her as well. And had asked her to marry him. And, while she was still not completely convinced about the being married bit…

"Maggie, stop thinking," Thomas ordered.

Maggie's last thought, which avoided the statistical rigour an academic would usually apply to such statements, was that she was sure she was the happiest woman on earth.

Sometime later, Maggie was drinking coffee in her study when there was a knock on the door. It opened to Gweneth Conyers, a very pretty blonde who was married to Thomas' oldest son and heir, William. William was a barrister and lived with Gweneth and their two children in nearby Cheltenham.

"Why hello, Gweneth."

"Hello, Maggie."

"Are you here with William? And the children?"

"Um, no. Just me."

Maggie was surprised. Gweneth had never visited on her own before. At least while Maggie had been at Beaumatin. Which admittedly had not been all that long.

"Would you like some tea? Coffee?"

"I saw Mrs Cook. She's bringing in some tea, thank you."

Gweneth looked around the room.

"This is very nice. I like what you've done with it. It must be a pleasant place to work."

When she had arrived at Beaumatin, Maggie had found the room she used as a study awash in chintz in pinks and blues, the way Harriet had left it. It was undeniably lovely but not really Maggie's style. She had redecorated it using a William Morris wallpaper in greens and rusts. And filled the lower half of the walls with bookcases that were now crammed full of books, academic journals and other research materials. A study for a painting by Dante Gabriel Rossetti hung over the fireplace. The picture of a woman with masses of auburn curls reminded Maggie of her own.

"Yes, it is," Maggie agreed.

Mrs Cook came in. A pleasantly plump woman in her fifties, she had curly grey hair and wore a starched white apron over a light blue cotton dress. She served Gweneth's tea, poured some fresh coffee for Maggie and then left.

"So…" Maggie began.

"Um. How much do you know about what's been planned for the wedding?"

"Constance's wedding? Virtually nothing."

In fact, Maggie felt like she was expected to be like Harry Potter at the Dursleys, when he said, "And I of course will be in my room, making no noise and pretending that I don't exist."

"That's what William was afraid of. Constance. That girl. Really. Anyway, he thought it would be a good idea if I briefed you about what to expect."

"What to expect," Maggie echoed.

"The von Fersens. Nils' family. They're staying here with you at Beaumatin."

"Yes." This Maggie had known.

"There are ten of them, in addition to Nils." Gweneth pulled a sheet of paper from her handbag and handed it to Maggie.

"Ten?" echoed Maggie faintly. Oh dear. She had thought three or four.

"Does Mrs Cook know?"

"Constance told her. And about who should go in which room."

"Oh."

Maggie looked at the list. It had been prettily hand-written by Gweneth.

Georg Axel von Fersen, Father

Ulrika Gyllenborg von Fersen, Father's mother

Anna Sofia Bielke von Fersen, Mother

Franz Gustaf Bielke, Uncle (Mother's brother)

Carl Magnus von Fersen, Uncle (Father's brother)

Elisabeth von Vexküll von Fersen, Uncle's wife

Fredrik Otto von Fersen, Brother (older)

Margaretha Stackelberg von Fersen, Brother's wife

Agneta Von Fersen Ekeblad, Sister (older)

Erich Konstantin Ekeblad, Sister's husband

"Um. Do they speak English, do you know?"

"I think most of them, yes."

"Most of them."

"According to Constance, the von Fersens are an old, distinguished family. Swedish nobility. And Nil's uncle, Franz Bielke, is a much-decorated diplomat. He's now retired."

"All right. Besides offering them the kind of hospitality I would any guest, is there anything special I should know?"

Gweneth looked thoughtful.

"I don't think so. Constance has been to Sweden and met them. She didn't mention anything."

"No vegans? Recovering alcoholics? Allergies to animals or lactose? Bi-polar disorders?"

Gweneth laughed. "No. At least not as far as I'm aware. Based on what Constance said."

"Does Thomas know? That there are going to be this many people?"

Gweneth made a face.

"I don't know."

"Well, I'm sure we can cope for a few days."

"A few days? Oh dear. You really have no idea?"

"Um, no. Tell me."

Maggie was now alarmed.

"The von Fersen contingent is arriving on the seventeenth and staying through New Year's. I think Constance said everyone is going back on January second."

"What? But that's…" Maggie did some quick arithmetic. "Two weeks. More than two weeks. Sixteen days. Are they staying here the whole time? Don't they want to spend some time in London? Or take the Eurostar to Paris for a day or two?"

"I think Constance has planned some day trips," said Gweneth vaguely.

Maggie was aghast. This would be her and Thomas' first Christmas together. She had expected to see his sons, William and James, and their families. But now it looked like they would have a whole house full of people who were strangers. And for New Year's as well.

And Thomas was not very, well, social. In fact he tended to be a bit of a recluse. He was fine with people he knew, like the Ainswicks, and some of Maggie's friends from Oxford. But otherwise…

"Constance has everything well planned." Gweneth was trying to be reassuring.

"She's talked to Ned about organising some shooting and she is getting in extra horses if people want to ride. And apparently she and Mrs Cook have all the menus arranged, so you needn't worry about cooking."

Maggie told herself she needed to get a grip.

"It seems that Constance has been busy," she finally said.

Gweneth seemed relieved that Maggie was taking the news so well.

"And then William thought you might want to be briefed on the protocol for the wedding."

"Protocol? It's a wedding, right? Bride's side, groom's side. Ushers walk you up the aisle. You stand when the bride enters, stand when she leaves. It's the same church where Thomas and I got married, isn't it? The same vicar? The same service?"

"Well, yes, you're right. It's the same church. But…"

Gweneth took some folded sheets of paper from her handbag and gave them to Maggie.

"This is the guest list."

Wolcum Yole

Maggie looked at pages of names.

"Can the church seat this many people?"

"Yes. Just. If everyone squeezes in."

Maggie was skimming through the list. She knew the Ainswicks. Their daughter Chloe and her husband David Osborne. The Nesbitts. The Sumners. Simon Peevey and his fiancée. Everyone else was a stranger. There were quite a few Sirs and Ladies, some Lords and Ladies, and…

"And those are the royals." Gweneth pointed.

"Royals?"

"Yes. He's, like, umpteenth in line for the throne."

"Oh."

"You curtsy when you're presented."

"Curtsy?"

"Yes," said Gweneth, like Maggie was being very dim.

"Oh. I sometimes forget. You're American."

"Um, could you show me?"

"All right." Gweneth seemed to think this was a strange request but was going to humour Maggie.

She demonstrated.

Maggie tried and tottered.

"Oh dear. Well, I'll practice and hope I don't fall on my face."

"That would not be good," Gweneth said emphatically.

"Anything else?"

"There'll be a receiving line after the ceremony. Since you're Lady Raynham, you'll be in it."

"All right. I've done receiving lines before. Unless there's something different I should know."

"No. You just need to remember to curtsy. To the royals. Not to anyone else, though."

"Curtsy. Right."

Maggie thought.

"Was your wedding like this?"

"Oh, it was much bigger. Because of William's being the heir. And my mother is a Symeon."

Maggie knew Symeon was the Ainswick's family name. Lord Ainswick was Gweneth's uncle.

"So thankful for small blessings?"

Gweneth looked confused at that but smiled anyway.

After Gweneth had left, Maggie went to find Thomas.

He was in his study.

"Do you have a moment?" she asked.

"Of course," he smiled and his bright blue eyes were warm.

Maggie smiled back and nearly lost her train of thought.

"Yes?"

"Oh. Sorry." She sat in a chair beneath another painting by Dante Gabriel Rossetti that hung over the fireplace. It was of a woman brushing her long, curly auburn hair. Maggie knew it reminded Thomas of her. Or vice versa.

"How much do you know about Constance's plans for her wedding?"

Thomas shrugged. He glanced at a calendar.

"I know it's the twenty-second. And that Constance has organised some sort of do here that evening."

"And you know Nils' family are staying here."

"Er… I seem to remember something…"

Maggie handed him the list Gweneth had given her.

"There are ten of them. Plus, I assume, Constance and Nils."

Thomas frowned.

"Ten?"

"Yes."

"Plus Constance and Nils?"

"Yes."

He sighed.

"All right. Well. Anything else?"

"Only that the von Fersens are arriving at Beaumatin on the seventeenth. And are staying here until January second."

"What?"

"Sixteen days. Which include Christmas and New Year's."

Thomas' frown had become a scowl.

"Did you know anything about this?" Maggie asked.

"No."

"Well, neither did I. Until a few minutes ago. When thankfully William sent Gweneth over to, er, appraise me of Constance's plans."

From Thomas' look, Maggie decided that it was lucky for Constance that she was not there or she might have gotten spanked.

Thomas sighed. "Well, Papillon, I'm afraid there's not much we can do about it now."

He looked at his calendar again.

"We have a week to ourselves, it seems. We'll just have to make the most of it."

Wolcum Yole

Chapter 3

The week passed blissfully but all too quickly. Maggie welcomed the predictable routine of life at Beaumatin. They rode. They snuggled while Thomas watched the History channel. She cooked. Anticipating sixteen days of pies and roasts and other traditional fare—would there be a Christmas turkey? Or even a Dickensian goose?—Maggie made an Italian butternut squash lasagne. A bordello pink beet risotto with goat cheese and, to soften the shock for Thomas, chicken cutlets Milanese. A seafood stew. Chili with cornmeal dumplings. Chinese chicken with cashew nuts.

Busy with preparations for the descent of the von Fersens and the wedding festivities that would be held at Beaumatin, Mrs Cook was happy to be relieved of some of her kitchen duties.

Late on Saturday the fifteenth, Constance and Nils arrived. Constance was blonde and lovely. Maggie assumed she resembled her mother. Nils was blond and handsome and obviously a man deeply in love.

A simple supper was dominated by Constance telling her father about her plans. Maggie and Nils were a captive audience and it was Maggie's impression that Thomas was not listening very attentively, but she kept this to herself.

The next morning Constance and Nils attended church and met with the vicar following the service. Constance spent the rest of the day with Mrs Cook and continued with her planning. She ignored Maggie.

Maggie and Thomas took a long ride in the afternoon. Maggie rode Dido, a gentle chestnut mare, while Thomas rode Troubadour, a spirited, dappled grey stallion.

"If I were a runner preparing for a marathon, today is the day I'd be carbo-loading. I guess in this case I'm Thomas-loading," she decided.

The Swedes, as Maggie was thinking collectively of the von Fersen delegation, since she knew none of them individually as yet, arrived as planned late in the afternoon on the seventeenth. William, who was in his mid-thirties and looked like a younger version of his father, and Gweneth had come over earlier to be part of the welcoming party.

Constance and Nils had gone to Heathrow airport to meet his family and had accompanied them back in three large black Mercedes vans—people carriers Maggie had heard them called.

Maggie and Thomas and the Conyers went out to greet the arrivals.

First to clamber out was Nils. He turned and helped out a man and woman in their mid-sixties.

"Nils parents?" Maggie wondered. If so, that would be Georg Axel and Anna Sofia. She had tried to memorize everyone's name and occupation. It was hard for her without any faces to associate with them, but she had done her best.

The man was wearing a well-tailored camel overcoat, the woman a lush mink, nearly black in the fading winter light. The woman was carefully made up and had immaculately styled short blonde hair. The man's hair was slightly darker and thinning. Both had the look of people who were ready to be done with travelling for the day.

The man turned back to the van and helped down an elderly woman. She had snowy white hair gathered back in a bun, wore a long dark wool coat and used an ebony cane.

Wolcum Yole

This must be Nils' grandmother, Ulrika von Fersen, Maggie decided. The woman looked to be in her late eighties. She did not smile but stood ramrod straight as she regarded the great house with its eccentric architectural mix.

Out of the second van came another couple. In their late fifties, Maggie guessed. This must be Georg Axel's younger brother, Carl Magnus, and his wife Elisabeth. The von Fersen brothers looked remarkably alike, except for the difference in age. Elisabeth von Fersen, however, was an attractive brunette, an anomaly amidst the von Fersen blondness. Maggie immediately related. All of the Raynham women were also blondes.

A younger couple emerged next. This was either Nils' brother or his sister and his or her spouse. Maggie looked for a family resemblance but could not be sure. One thing was certain, however. The woman was pregnant. While Maggie was no expert, she guessed in the second trimester. But the von Fersens were all tall and thin, so perhaps she was further along.

The doors of the third van opened. Another younger couple got out. Early thirties. Nils' brother? Sister? Maggie decided she would have to wait for introductions.

Constance climbed out, looking somewhat flustered. Last to disembark was a man in his mid-sixties with long, white-blond hair swept back. He wore a black cashmere overcoat with a long white silk scarf.

"Lucius Malfoy from Harry Potter," was Maggie's immediate reaction. He was still quite handsome, but haughty, with icy blue eyes, high cheekbones and a scar that ran down the right side of his face.

"Was that a duelling scar?" Maggie wondered and then reminded herself it was more likely from a childhood playground accident.

Maggie concluded this was Franz Bielke, the ambassador, and Nils' mother's brother. He looked bored and removed a gold cigarette case from an inside pocket. He opened it, took out a fancy cigarette wrapped in black paper with a golden filter tip, and lit it with a heavy gold cigarette lighter.

The vans' drivers unloaded the von Fersens' luggage and took off. A stringy man in his fifties appeared. It was Ned, the Beaumatin foreman. He brought with him Ian and Wesley, who worked on the grounds of the estate. They began to carry the suitcases into the house.

Thomas indicated that the new arrivals should enter the house. They followed him through a massive oak door centred in a Georgian façade beneath a coat of arms carved in stone. At the bottom was scrolled the Raynham motto, "Numquam cede," which Maggie knew meant "Never give up" or "We never yield."

The group came into the great hall with its ancestral portraits hanging over settees and tables in oak so old they were black. At the end of the space a grand staircase rose up one flight to a landing, then a second flight went up to the floor above.

The group looked around and took in the baronial grandeur. Carl Magnus gaped, Anna Sofia nodded in satisfaction and nudged her husband and Maggie noticed Constance trying not to look smug.

Constance performed the introductions. She grudgingly included Maggie with "and this is my father's wife." Her hostility towards Maggie was obvious and Maggie repressed an urge to slap her.

Maggie found out she had been correct about who Nils' parents and grandmother were. Nil's father, Georg Axel, was a retired judge and still carried an air of judicial authority. Nils' mother, Anna Sofia, worked in the Ministry of Culture. Something to do with museums, if Maggie remembered Gweneth's briefing correctly.

Carl Magnus, Nils' uncle, was a retired banker and his wife Elisabeth was a professor of French at Stockholm University. Maggie hoped this would give them something else in common, in addition to neither's being blonde.

The pregnant woman was Nils' sister, Agneta von Fersen Ekeblad, married to Erich. Agneta was a lawyer and her husband Erich worked in another government ministry. Was it commerce? It had something to do with business. Maggie decided she would ask. She would certainly be spending enough time with these people.

This meant the couple from the third van were Nils' brother Fredrik and his wife, Margaretha. Fredrik, Maggie seemed to recall, was an architect and his wife was in publishing.

"Begin as you mean to go on," Maggie reminded herself. So she shook hands, smiled graciously and welcomed Nils' family to her home. Constance scowled.

"Tough tuna," thought Maggie. "And it is my home. Kind of."

When she was introduced to Bielke, the ambassador, she extended her hand and, to her embarrassment, he raised it to his lips and kissed it as he bowed slightly.

"Good grief," was Maggie's reaction.

The von Fersens were being cool and polite. The Raynhams were also being cool and polite. Maggie wondered about all the coolness and if it had to do with social position and breeding.

She imagined names for the children. Constance's and Nils' as well as Agneta's. Icicle. Glacier. Hoarfrost. Frostbite. Iceberg. Frigidity. Anna Arctica. Chilly Willy. Now she was becoming silly and hoped that at least she was exuding some warmth. Everyone was here for a wedding. It should be a joyous occasion.

Mrs Cook came and was introduced. Suitcases were identified, coats were collected and Constance said she would show people to their rooms. Ian, Wesley and Ned assisted with carrying the suitcases. Given the length of their stay, the Swedes had at least two apiece.

Thomas proposed that, after people settled in their rooms, they meet for cocktails in the drawing room in half an hour.

Escorted by Constance, the von Fersens trooped off upstairs. Gweneth went back to the kitchen with Mrs Cook and William went into the library to take a call on his mobile.

Maggie and Thomas looked at each other. He hugged her.

"Mon pauvre papillon. It's only two weeks. Well sixteen days, but we're already through most of the first day. We'll survive."

Maggie wondered whether Thomas was trying to comfort her or himself.

Chapter 4

Constance, with Nils' assistance, had researched his family's drink preferences and Mrs Cook had set up a bar in the drawing room. Most of the men were drinking their choice of Thomas' selection of whiskies. The women varied from vodka to champagne, while Agneta had apple juice. Maggie was drinking Viognier, her new white wine of choice. Elisabeth, the brunette, joined her.

"This is nice," the woman said. Maggie was not sure whether she was referring to the wine, the family gathering or the room, which Maggie estimated was bigger than her entire flat in Oxford. It had an ornately plastered ceiling from which hung elaborate crystal chandeliers and half a dozen seating areas that were organised around some fine Aubusson carpets. Portraits of the barons, their wives and children and, frequently, their horses and dogs, were displayed on walls covered with rich yellow brocade, and a painting by John Constable hung over a large, marble-fronted fireplace.

Maggie looked around. Excluding Thomas and William, she felt as though she and Elisabeth were ducks in a flock of swans. But then again, she was wearing her favourite ruffled black leather jacket with tight black pants and an ivory satin shell and all in all felt very kickass.

"Bring it on, swans," she thought.

There was a lull in the conversation. Margaretha, Nils' sister-in-law, turned to Maggie and said in heavily accented English, "Constance said you are a teacher, yes?"

With everyone looking at her, Maggie rapidly pondered whether she should explain that she was a professor at Oxford or assume the wording was the result of a limited command of English and simply say, "Yes."

However, before she could respond, a bored voice said, "Really, Netta. Don't you know Lady Raynham is also Professor Margaret Spence Eliot, a distinguished fellow at Oxford University? She just published a rather controversial book. You can see some of her interviews on YouTube. They can be quite entertaining."

It was Franz Bielke. Maggie thought he was looking more Lucius Malfoy than ever in a fashionably cut black wool suit, white shirt and black tie. Armani? Versace? Zegna? It had certainly not come from one of the British tailors that Thomas and William patronised.

With everyone staring at her, Bielke continued. He addressed himself to Maggie.

"And I understand you have another book coming out in early January."

"Yes. It covers the same topic as the current book. But is written for a wider audience."

"Ah Franz. You always know everything." It was Nils' mother, Anna Sofia. She was wearing an elegant suit in sky blue wool and was even more immaculately groomed than when she had arrived. Not a hair was out of place. Maggie briefly wondered what the woman thought of her own out-of-control curls.

Anna Sofia turned to Maggie and asked. "You are a writer, then?"

She continued before Maggie could answer. "I have always wanted to write. Fiction. Like *Män som hatar kvinnor*. You know? Stieg Larsson?"

"The Girl with the Dragon Tattoo?" Maggie guessed the obvious.

"Yes. That one. But my books would be less dark. Not so ugly."

Georg Axel looked at his wife in disbelief, while Bielke's expression was easily recognized by Maggie as, "Yeah, right."

While Maggie thought about something neutral to say, Mrs Cook came in to tell her that dinner was ready to be served.

Before people could begin a third round of drinks, Maggie stood and suggested they all move to the dining room, whose pale blue walls were also hung with Raynham ancestors.

There were sixteen at dinner, the most since Maggie had been at Beaumatin. She blessed Mrs Cook for having figured out who should sit where and putting out place cards. Maggie found that Franz Bielke was on her right and Georg Axel von Fersen was on her left. At the far end of the table, Thomas had Ulrika von Fersen on his right and Anna Sofia on his left. Constance and Nils sat opposite each other in the middle.

Mrs Griggs and Mrs Bateson, two local women who helped Mrs Cook with the housework, had been recruited for the duration of the von Fersens' visit and helped serve and clear the dinner, which was cauliflower stilton soup, roast venison and apple crumble.

Georg Axel tended to be taciturn and addressed himself to his soup, roast and pudding. Maggie was thankful when Franz Bielke picked up the conversational ball and entertained Gweneth, who was sitting on his right, and her with anecdotes from his various embassy postings. Elisabeth, who was sitting next to Georg Axel, was less amused.

"Perhaps she has heard these stories before," Maggie thought.

Conversation in the middle of the table was a mix of Swedish and English. Nils acted as a translator. Constance had been trying to learn Swedish but was still far from being fluent. Except for Bielke's tales, conversation was general—the weather, the flight from Stockholm, airport security, the weather.

The von Fersens were not inclined to self-revelation and seemed to lack much curiosity about their hosts. Or the several barons whose portraits watched over the diners.

With the meal over, Thomas proposed after-dinner drinks and William challenged Fredrik and Erich to join him and Nils for a game of billiards. The ladies were of course welcome to come and provide support.

Bielke turned to Maggie. "I need a cigarette and I notice no one in this house seems to smoke. It's a disgusting habit, I know. So I will go outside. Would you care to join me?"

Maggie shook her head. "Thank you, but I am doubtless needed here. However, I am sure I will see you again shortly."

"Of course." Bielke bowed and left.

Elisabeth was standing next to Maggie.

"An interesting man," Maggie commented.

"Don't find him too interesting." Elisabeth was solemn.

"Is there a Mrs Bielke?" Maggie was curious.

"There have been three."

"Three? Really?"

"I doubt there will be a fourth. Franz has found other ways to... amuse himself."

"Oh?"

"I shouldn't be saying this, but... don't trust him. You're exactly the sort of woman he..."

"Oh. Just because he can tell amusing stories hardly means I would... Besides, Thomas..."

"You think so now."

This was very strange, Maggie thought. She smiled and said, "I believe there is some of that nice Viognier left. Can I interest you in joining me with a glass?"

Later, after their guests had all gone off to bed, Maggie was in her room. She found entertaining people who were not actual friends exhausting. She was just about to undress and put on her nightgown when there was a light knocking at her door.

It was Thomas.

"Time for bed. Come," he said.

Maggie smiled. "All right. Just let me..." she reached out for the nightgown she had laid on the bed.

"You won't need that," he said.

Susan Alexander

Chapter 5

"Shooting. Constance has organised a shooting party. Since it's not raining for once. At least that's the plan," Maggie told Thomas.

Thomas grimaced. Maggie knew he had not done any shooting since his father had been killed in a hunting accident a quarter of a century earlier.

"My dear, would you mind terribly…"

"Of course not. I expect you have work you'd like to do. And I believe William is also coming. To support the Raynham side. Assuming we need support. Do any of the Swedes know how to shoot, do you think, or should the sheep be moved to a more distant pasture?"

Thomas smiled. Maggie kissed him on top of his head and prepared to do her duty as hostess.

It seemed that Georg Axel, Carl Magnus and Erich Ekeblad were joining the party. Franz Bielke admitted he had done some shooting and would also come along. Constance had organised a trip to Cheltenham for the ladies, but as Elisabeth confessed to still being tired from yesterday's journey, she said she would also join and watch the fun. At the last minute, Nils and Fredrik decided to come as well.

The participants sorted themselves between Ned's. William's and Maggie's Land Rovers and they took off to where Wesley and Ian had already set up several traps.

Erich had limited experience with shotguns and Nils and Fredrik, none. Maggie watched Ned give them a quick tutorial. Georg Axel and Carl Magnus hunted and said they were proficient. Bielke looked bored like he apparently always did and said he was sure he would be all right.

It turned out that Bielke was nearly as good a shot as William, who was the county champion, and Georg Axel was also proficient. Carl Magnus had overestimated his abilities, while Erich, Fredrik and Nils needed continuing coaching by the patient Ned.

When it came to Maggie's turn, Bielke walked over to her.

"Let me show you the correct stance," he said and went to put his arms around her to position the shotgun.

Maggie stepped away.

"Thank you, but I'm sure I'll be fine."

"Pull," she quickly told Ian.

Ian grinned and let off a fast double. Maggie blasted both to bits.

Bielke looked momentarily annoyed before he managed to mask his feelings with a slick smile.

"My, my. Impressive."

Maggie heard William telling the others about her just missing out on being a member of the US Olympic shooting team when she was in college.

Elisabeth said that she would like to try. Bielke quickly shifted his attention to the other woman and gave her pointers while Carl Magnus watched good-naturedly. The diplomat ignored Maggie for the rest of the outing.

Wolcum Yole

"Silly man. Does he think he's punishing me? Or trying to make me jealous?" Maggie wondered.

On the ride back, Bielke made sure to sit in the front of Maggie's Land Rover. He looked at her consideringly.

"Who would have thought a serious professor could also be a crack shot?"

Maggie shrugged. "It makes a nice change from reading academic journals."

"Do you hunt?"

"No. Although I've shot a few people," she added.

Bielke was taken aback.

"They deserved it," she said simply.

When the cars drew up in front of the house, Thomas came out. Bielke quickly got out, opened Maggie's door and helped her down, cutting off Thomas who was coming to perform the same courtesy.

"Thank you," said Maggie coolly to Bielke. She turned and beamed at Thomas.

"I believe the herds escaped without casualties."

Thomas nodded.

The group had a late lunch. Nils proposed people entertain themselves until the ladies returned.

Maggie went to her study to answer some emails and catch up on what was being posted about her book on the blogosphere. There was a knock on her door. She expected to see Thomas, but it was Bielke.

"Yes?"

"I wondered if you had a copy of your book that I could read."

"It's rather academic," she warned him.

"But it's caused so much controversy."

"I suspect some of its biggest critics didn't make it past the introduction."

"Well I've been to university. And your Kennedy School of Government. I'm sure I'll manage."

"Very well." Maggie walked over and pulled a copy from a bookshelf and handed it to Bielke.

"No autograph?" he teased.

Thomas came in. He looked at Maggie and Bielke standing together and frowned slightly.

"Ambassador Bielke asked if he could borrow a copy of my book. I suspect he is having trouble sleeping and thinks this will help."

Thomas nodded, frosty. Bielke looked amused.

"Thank you, Lady Raynham," he said and left.

"I just had a call from Constance. She expects they will be out for another two hours or so. I got the impression some of the ladies want to stop at a tea shop for an English cream tea. I need to go out with Ned. Can you manage?"

Maggie sighed. "Couldn't I come with you?"

Thomas thawed slightly.

Wolcum Yole

"I'm not sure that would be fair to Mrs Cook."

"You're right, of course. And yes, I'll manage."

"And tomorrow is the day trip to Oxford. I assume you're acting as tour guide?"

"Um, no. I was not invited."

Thomas looked surprised.

Maggie had also thought this was strange, as Constance had defied family tradition by studying medicine at Cambridge and then epidemiology at the University of London. But, whatever.

"Anyway, no worries. I'll man the gates."

Thomas kissed her, started to become distracted, then resolutely stepped away.

Maggie worked undisturbed for over an hour. She was replying to an email from her publisher when she heard a noise in the hall and went out to investigate.

It was a stranger. He was tall, a few inches taller than Maggie's 5'11" and had a round, bald head whose scalp shone except for a strip of steely grey that curved around the back from ear to ear. Overweight, with his stomach protruding over his trousers, he had chubby-cheeks that were flushed, a button nose and a sensuous mouth. Somewhere between sixty and seventy—Maggie found it hard to guess his age—the man was wearing a loud houndstooth tweed jacket in greens and browns that would never have been found in Thomas' closet, pants that failed to match and a beige V-neck pullover over a dress shirt.

Light grey eyes stared out from behind thin-framed glasses and took in the great hall with its ancestral portrait gallery.

"Hello. May I help you?"

He looked Maggie over. In her casual navy wool slacks, ivory fisherman's sweater and loafers, and her hair pulled back with a hairclip, the stranger apparently decided she was household help.

"I'm here to see Miss Conyers. Miss Constance Conyers."

"Yes. And you are?"

"She's expecting me."

His tone was peremptory.

"What a jerk," thought Maggie.

"Yes. And exactly whom is Miss Conyers expecting?" she asked again, with an edge to her voice.

Head to one side, the stranger was contemplating a portrait of the eighth baron and did not answer.

Just then, Maggie was surprised but pleased to see William come strolling out from the back of the house. He looked at the man and raised his eyebrows.

Maggie shrugged.

"This… person is asking for Constance. He says he's expected. But is disinclined to identify himself."

Maggie felt like William was channelling Thomas. He looked the newcomer over, decided he was not impressed, and said, "Perhaps Mrs Cook knows something. I'll ask her."

Maggie was left with the man. Normally she would have invited a visitor to wait in the drawing room, but decided that, since he was being so rude, he could wait in the hall.

The man was fuming.

William returned with Mrs Cook. The housekeeper obviously had no idea who the man was.

"I'm sorry, Lady Raynham…" Mrs Cook began.

"Lady Raynham?" Suddenly the stranger's attitude was transformed.

"Lady Raynham, please forgive me. I'm Lionel Trueblood-Fitch. I've come to cover the Conyers-von Fersen wedding."

"Cover the wedding?"

"Yes. For *Country Style* magazine."

"*Country Style* magazine?" Maggie echoed.

She glanced at William. If there were one thing Thomas would hate more than having to entertain a house full of strangers, it would be having a reporter on the premises. Thomas shunned publicity.

"You're a journalist?" demanded William.

"A rapporteur," said Trueblood-Fitch pretentiously.

At that moment there were sounds of crashing and banging. The front door opened and another man entered, burdened with half a dozen bags and cases.

Maggie stared. The man was slim, of medium height, with short, chestnut, fur-like hair, dark beady eyes, a pointy nose, prominent front teeth and ears like a doll's tea cups. He had deep circles around his eyes.

"He looks just like a ferret," Maggie thought.

"This is Knowles. He's my photographer."

"Photographer?"

"Yes," said Trueblood-Fitch, beginning to sound impatient. "You're having a wedding, aren't you? Having a photographer is normal."

"Oh. You're the people from that magazine Miss Constance told me to expect," Mrs Cook said.

"Ah. At last." Trueblood-Fitch smiled to indicate his pleasure that someone had finally understood.

"And you're going to do an article on the wedding?" William demanded.

"The wedding will be featured in our Noteworthy Events section. The main article will be called 'Christmas at Beaumatin.'"

Trueblood-Fitch looked around the hall.

"Although I must admit I thought things would look a little more, well, like Christmas."

"Does my father know about this?" William asked Maggie.

"I don't know. He didn't say anything to me. And you know how he feels about publicity. But Constance really didn't tell either of us much about her plans."

"I wonder why," William muttered.

At that moment Thomas came in, still dressed for riding. He took in the scene.

"Yes?"

Maggie hoped Thomas wasn't going to shoot the messenger.

"This is Mr Trueblood-Fitch. And his photographer. Er, Knowles. He says they're here to cover the wedding for his magazine, *Country Style*. And to do an article. Christmas at Beaumatin. Constance…"

The front door opened and Constance and the von Fersens came in.

"Miss Conyers. I'm so glad to see you." Lionel was effusive.

"Oh. Hi, Lionel. Sorry not to have been here when you arrived. I was out."

Thomas was grim.

"Constance. We need to talk."

"All right. But first…"

"No. Now. My study."

Constance pouted but followed her father. Almost immediately there were muffled sounds of shouting.

Franz Bielke came out of the library holding Maggie's book. He looked at Trueblood-Fitch and Knowles, shook his head, and retreated.

"Mr Trueblood-Fitch? Mr Knowles? Why don't you wait in the drawing room until this is straightened out. Perhaps you would like some tea or coffee?"

Maggie was trying to get the situation under control. She noticed the von Fersens were looking on in varying degrees of disapproval.

"Would any of you care for some tea or coffee as well?"

Ulrika von Fersen sniffed. "No thank you. We just had some tea. I intend to rest before dinner. Anna Sofia, Margaretha, Agneta, don't you also wish to freshen up?"

The von Fersen women obediently followed Ulrika up the stairs to their rooms.

Mrs Cook went back to the kitchen, Bielke retreated to the library and Maggie and William were left alone in the hall. Sounds of sobbing were now coming from Thomas' study.

"It's only been two days. And we have two more weeks of this. I'm not sure your father will survive it. I'm not sure I'll survive it. What was Constance thinking?" Maggie asked William.

"I think she wanted to show off for the von Fersens. And, if I'm being honest, make things difficult for you."

"And this journalist? Trueblood-Fitch?"

Thomas' study was quiet.

"I assume he's about to get the boot," was William's assessment.

Wolcum Yole

But he was almost immediately proven wrong, as a very harassed-looking Thomas appeared, followed by a puffy-eyed, red-nosed Constance who nonetheless was smirking triumphantly.

"Where's this reporter?" Thomas demanded.

"In the drawing room," Maggie said.

Thomas went in and closed the door.

William glared at his sister.

Constance sniffed. "It's my wedding. I don't see what it has to do with you," she said to William. "And especially with you," she told Maggie.

Maggie was speechless, while she sensed William was counting down before he exploded. Very like his father, she thought.

Thomas came out of the drawing room.

"I assume you have arranged rooms for these… men with Mrs Cook. But they're eating in the kitchen with Ned and the others, not in the dining room. And I have veto rights on everything before it's published. Are we clear?"

Constance looked like she was going to argue.

"Nothing appears without my explicit approval or they're leaving now."

"Oh. Very well. All right."

Constance flounced into the drawing room.

Thomas glared at Maggie and William.

"Not one word," he warned and went back to his study.

Chapter 6

The next morning, after breakfast, the black vans reappeared to take everyone to Oxford for the day. Maggie sighed with relief as they drove down the drive and out of sight. She was still standing in front of the house when two pickup trucks appeared. The signs on the sides read, "Fiske and Hawking. Gardens." It was Derek and Damien.

"Hi guys. Come to deck the halls?" Maggie asked.

The back of one truck was loaded with Christmas trees in a range of sizes and rolled-up boughs of fir. The second truck carried an enormous Christmas tree and a few dozen large cardboard boxes.

"We have so many fairy lights, satellites will be able to pick out Beaumatin from space," said Derek proudly.

"Except they'll mostly be inside the house," Damien reminded him.

"I wanted to put lights on the trees that line the drive," Derek pointed out. "But there were problems with getting enough electricity."

"So they'll only be in the bough that is going to frame your front door," Damien finished.

"Oh dear," was Maggie's reaction. While she always had a Christmas tree, she tended to take a low-key approach to Christmas decorations.

While the men unloaded, Maggie went to see Mrs Cook to get another cup of coffee and to alert her to the presence of Derek and Damien. She found Trueblood-Fitch and Knowles finishing breakfast in the kitchen. Trueblood-Fitch was wearing another aggressively-woven checked tweed jacket in racing car yellow and royal blue while Knowles was looking as ferret-like as ever in jeans and a brown sweater.

Trueblood-Fitch stood.

"Lady Raynham. Good morning."

"Good morning." Maggie tried to be polite.

"Do I understand the men are coming today to start decorating for the wedding?"

"Yes. They just arrived."

"Good. Good. And everyone else has taken off to Oxford?"

"Yes. A day trip."

"In the meantime. I asked Lord Raynham. But he is busy. So I wondered. If you had the time. If you could give me a tour of your famous gardens?"

"It's December. There's really not much to see."

"But I understand you have an outstanding collection of cornus. And some of the early snowdrops are blooming…"

Maggie had been looking forward to a von-Fersen-free day. Even to spending some time with Thomas. She tried to smile.

"All right. In half an hour, then?"

"Thank you so much."

Maggie left with her mug of coffee. In the hall, she found Derek and Damien's trucks had been unloaded with the assistance of Ian and Wesley.

Derek was standing with his hands on his hips, looking at everything and seeming slightly panicked. He was wearing tight jeans and a black, body-hugging long-sleeved knit shirt.

Derek was buff, Maggie decided.

"What do we do first, Day?"

"Get the trees into their stands so they can get some water, Derek."

"Oh. You're so right. As usual."

Maggie had not realised that she had been followed by Trueblood-Fitch and Knowles.

"My goodness. It seems like you boys have your work cut out for you," said Trueblood-Fitch, eyeing Derek.

Damien looked at Trueblood-Fitch and decided he was underwhelmed. He glanced at Maggie.

"Um, Derek Fiske, Damien Hawking, this is Lionel Trueblood-Fitch. And, er, Knowles. Mr Trueblood-Fitch is from *Country Style* magazine and is here to cover the wedding. Knowles is his photographer."

Knowles smiled. It was not attractive.

"Call me Lionel," said Trueblood-Fitch, shaking hands. "I hope it's all right if we take some photographs while you decorate. I'm sure our readers would be interested. Before. During. After."

"As long as we get to see them first. And can make sure our names are spelled correctly," Damien insisted.

"We've had some bad experiences. And people tend to leave the 'e' off Fiske," Derek explained.

"Of course. Of course."

Well, Mr Trueblood-Fitch..." Maggie interjected.

"Please. Call me Lionel."

"Very well. Lionel. May I propose we meet here in twenty minutes for your garden tour?"

Lionel Trueblood-Fitch nodded and ambled back to the kitchen, followed by Knowles.

Maggie, Derek and Damien watched them go.

Damien turned to Derek.

"What's your gay-dar saying, Der?"

"Oh. Definitely."

Maggie was surprised. "Really? But he dresses so badly."

"That's stereotyping, Maggie. I'm surprised at you," said Derek sternly.

"Sorry."

"Perhaps he's colour blind," Damien offered.

"And what about Knowles?" Maggie asked.

"Knowles?"

"His photographer? Looks like a ferret?"

"A ferret. I knew he reminded me of something," Damien clapped his hand to his forehead.

"Yes. Anyhow, what does your, er, gay-dar say about him?"

Derek thought.

"I'm not getting a reading. He reminds me of that poor sod in the Bela Lugosi Dracula movie. Renford? Renfield? Dracula bites him and he spends the rest of the movie doing Dracula's bidding and begging for flies to eat."

"Or even better, Marty Feldman in *Young Frankenstein*. Remember Igor? Who scuttles around going 'Yes, Master. Yes, Master,'" Damien suggested.

Maggie laughed. "You guys are bad."

She went into her study to check her email. When it was time, she found Trueblood-Fitch waiting in the hall.

Maggie led the reporter to a room off the kitchen where jackets, hats, boots and other outdoor items were kept.

"There's been so much rain, the paths can be quite muddy. So I suggest boots," instructed Maggie as she pulled on a pair.

Trueblood-Fitch made a face and complied reluctantly.

Maggie tried to remember how Thomas showed the gardens to visitors and attempted to recreate one of his tours as closely as possible.

"Of course, as I said, there's not very much to see now. Just the winter skeleton of the gardens, in fact. The hamamelis, the witch hazel, are still a few weeks away from blooming. The cornus of course are adding some interest. I believe there are eight or nine different varieties."

They had reached one of the gardens farthest from the house.

"That's a cornus Arctic Sun, if I'm not mistaken," Maggie pointed to the bush with its brilliant yellow branches tipped with red.

But something else had caught Trueblood-Fitch's eye.

"Snowdrops? I thought they didn't bloom until February."

"These are very early flowering," Maggie explained.

"Pretty," replied Lionel vaguely. He was looking at something to the left of the Potter's Early and Peter Gatehouse and Barnes.

Maggie followed his gaze.

It was a solitary clump of snowdrops with four flowers. The outer segments were lightly streaked with pinstripes of green and the inner segments showed a pale green hourglass marking.

"Hmm. That's different," Maggie thought.

She realised she had lost Trueblood-Fitch's attention.

"Lionel?"

Lionel started.

"What?"

"That's about it. In terms of the gardens."

Lionel was looking around, as though he were trying to fix a location.

"Lionel?" Maggie prompted again.

"Hmm. Yes?"

"It's starting to rain. Perhaps we should go back. You've seen virtually everything."

"Oh. Of course."

They returned to the house.

They were back in what Maggie called the "mud room" to herself and were removing their boots.

"Well, thank you, Lady Raynham. I am sure Lord Raynham himself would not have been a better guide. And not been nearly so charming."

Trueblood-Fitch smiled an ingratiating smile.

Maggie gave a perfunctory smile in return. She didn't know why she disliked this man so much. Which was why she had not asked him to call her Maggie, even though the Lady Raynham-ing still tended to make her flinch. Inwardly anyhow.

What had Constance been thinking to have invited someone like him to come here? Of course, that was one in a long series of "What had Constance been thinkings?"

Maggie found Damien and Derek decorating a small forest of pine trees with fairy lights in the hall.

"Hi, guys. How's it going?" Maggie asked.

"Two thousand, nine hundred, seventeen fairy lights done, four thousand six hundred, eighty three more to go," said Damien.

"Oh dear. Well, at least that's some progress," said Maggie.

"I can tell you're a cup half-full kind of girl," said Derek.

"I've just never seen the point of viewing a cup as half-empty," Maggie agreed.

"Are you going to want lunch?" she asked.

"No. Thanks anyway. We need to check out how things are going back at the shop."

"Christmas trees? Poinsettias? Amaryllis? Wreaths?" asked Maggie.

"All of the above. And fairy lights, of course," said Derek.

"Charming," came another voice. It was Lionel Trueblood-Fitch.

"Hi Lionel," said Derek. "What do you think?"

Trueblood-Fitch put his head to one side and considered.

"I think that's a lot of fairy lights," he said finally.

"And that's not even half of them," said Damien.

"It's what Constance wanted," Derek reminded him.

"I know. But is the customer always right?" Damien asked.

Maggie said, "I'll leave you gentlemen to debate that one. I'll see you later."

She retreated to her study while the men continued to chat.

Maggie sighed. She answered a few emails. She skimmed through the day's news. Then she remembered the unusual snowdrop she had noticed. She couldn't recall there being an early snowdrop like that. She checked out a few sites that had extensive photo galleries of snowdrops. Nothing resembled the flower she had seen, with its green-streaked segments. At least none that bloomed before Christmas.

She retrieved her copy of the "Snowdrop Bible" which Thomas had given her from a bookcase. The famous work by Bishop, Davis and Grimshaw also had nothing that looked like what she had seen.

Maggie decided she would tell Thomas about it at lunch and take him to see it after they ate.

And thinking of lunch made Maggie notice the time. Oh dear. She was late. But then normally Thomas would have come to remind her. Perhaps he was late as well.

Maggie entered the dining room to find Thomas with Franz Bielke. The men stood.

"Ambassador Bielke. You didn't go to Oxford with the others?" Maggie asked in surprise.

"No. I'm no tourist. And failed to see the point if our distinguished professor were not going to act as a guide."

There was a bit of jostling as both men went to pull out Maggie's chair for her. Being closer, Thomas performed the courtesy. But he looked exasperated.

Lunch was Mrs Cook's famous butternut squash soup. Feeling the tension between the two men, Maggie was glad Thomas had opened a bottle of Puligny Montrachet.

Bielke was urbane and entertaining as usual. He recalled Christmases he had spent in places from Buenos Ares to Riyadh to Kuala Lumpur. Maggie listened politely and laughed when appropriate. Thomas, who had travelled little, became testy as his guest continued to dominate the conversation.

Thomas was not a raconteur, Maggie decided.

Declining pudding, Bielke glanced out a window.

"It seems your infernal rain has let up a bit. I understand there are horses and that riding is possible. May I ask if either of you have the time to act as an escort?" He looked at Maggie.

"I thought you weren't a tourist," Thomas reminded the man.

"It is true I don't find riding in a van oohing and aahing at historic monuments amusing. But exercise and some fresh air? Your lovely countryside? It can hardly be compared…"

"I'm afraid I have some work to do." Thomas was unapologetic.

"Then perhaps Lady Raynham…"

Maggie looked at Thomas. He shrugged.

Maggie sighed to herself.

"Can you be ready in an hour?"

"Certainly."

"Then I'll tell Ned," said Maggie, trying to sound more enthusiastic than she felt.

Bielke appeared promptly in a perfectly fitted black hacking jacket, white shirt with stock and creamy jodhpurs. Black riding boots gleamed and he carried a riding crop.

Maggie, who was wearing a waterproof blue riding jacket, breeches, a flannel shirt and well-worn boots, was taken aback. Yes, Bielke looked splendid but also somewhat silly for a ride in the country on a wet December day.

"More Lucius Malfoy than ever," she decided.

Ned was waiting in front of the house with Dido, the gentle chestnut mare Maggie normally rode, and Dexter, a black gelding who was one of the horses Constance had borrowed for her guests.

Maggie saw Ned look at Bielke and hide a smile. They exchanged glances.

Mounted, they set off. Maggie considered which route to take and decided to keep to the estate for the most part. For a second time that day she tried to mimic Thomas-as-tour-guide.

Surveying yet another field dotted with ewes and their lambs, Bielke turned to Maggie and asked, "So how are you finding it, being a country squire's wife? As opposed to being a controversial Oxford academic?"

Maggie was surprised. She had expected more of Bielke's entertaining anecdotes, which she supposed were part of a diplomat's stock-in-trade. And she certainly did not care for Bielke's referring to his host as a country squire.

"I'm enjoying both," she responded neutrally.

Bielke sat back on his horse and looked at her sceptically.

"Really? You don't find endless discussions about lambs and crops and the weather tedious compared to your Merrion high table?"

"In fact, lamb is just as likely to be a subject of conversation at the high table—whether it's been properly cooked and if a St Estephe wouldn't have complemented it better than the Haut Brion. It's not all geopolitics and monetary policy. And this is England. Everyone is always talking about the weather."

"I personally find the thought of another evening spent in the company of this group of dullards so unbearable, I'm tempted to steal one of those dreadful vans and drive straight to London. Can I persuade you join me?" Bielke's smile was seductive.

"Ambassador Bielke…" Maggie hoped he was joking.

"Please. Call me Franz."

Maggie hesitated.

"And may I call you Maggie? That is how you're called, isn't it? Not Margaret, I understand."

Maggie reluctantly nodded, to avoid seeming rude. She began to ride forward but Bielke put out his riding crop to stop her.

Maggie grabbed the crop and tried to gently push it back towards the man but he held it in place.

"I'm sorry?" she said stiffly.

"No. As I am sure there are only more fields with more sheep ahead. Let's stay and talk. I have been wanting to talk to you. You must realise you are the only interesting person in that monstrous pile you inhabit."

"I'm certain that's not true, Ambas... Franz," said Maggie in embarrassment.

"And I repeat my original question. About how you're finding it, being Lady Raynham. I couldn't help but notice that in your interviews are you invariably Professor Eliot."

"That is because I prefer to keep my professional and private lives separate."

"Really? Are you sure it's not also because you prefer being Professor Eliot to Lady Raynham? I notice you cringe when you're called that. Oh, don't worry. It isn't obvious. Just a flicker in your eyes. But it's there to see if someone cares to look for it."

"Oh dear," Maggie thought and hoped Thomas didn't notice. Then she stopped herself. Her problem wasn't Thomas, but Bielke. She had no desire to have this kind of conversation with the man.

Bielke was watching her closely.

"Or is it a case of marrying in haste, repenting at leisure? You could hardly have known Raynham very well when you married him, after all. Or realised how isolated life out in the country would be. With only sheep for neighbours. He is known for being a recluse, your husband. Although I can see how someone might have been dazzled by the idea of the title and the estate."

Maggie glared at Bielke.

"I was not dazzled by a title…" Maggie began while she thought that, in fact, it had been a pair of bright blue eyes she had found dazzling. But she was certainly not going to say that to this intrusive man.

"Your step-daughter, Constance, certainly thinks so. She was in Stockholm shortly after the wedding. Raving. She dislikes you intensely, you know. And she convinced my well-groomed but air-headed sister you were a fortune hunter."

Maggie laughed.

"Ambas… Franz. I have my own title and do not need anyone's fortune. And I know how Constance feels, as she's told me so herself. Although I'm sorry to hear she's so ill-mannered that she tells others as well.

"However, as it seems you have no interest in sheep and it has started to drizzle, I suggest we return. Because while my jacket is designed for our English weather, yours is not and it would be pity if it became too soggy."

Maggie backed up Dido a few paces and turned around, out of reach of Bielke's still outstretched riding crop.

"As you wish. But remember, sometimes talking to a sympathetic stranger…"

"Yes. And I understand you have rather extensive experience in the marital area," Maggie responded somewhat sharply.

Bielke's ice blue eyes became hard. Maggie imagined glaciers. He tried to hide his annoyance with a smile and said, "I wouldn't have thought you were someone who indulges in gossip."

Maggie shrugged. "I'm not. But Constance is not the only one here who is indiscrete."

She rode off. By the time they reached Beaumatin, the drizzle had become a steady rain and Bielke was quite wet.

Thomas was in the hall and took in Bielke, who was soaked, and Maggie, who was dry except for her curls, which had exploded in the damp. His mouth twitched.

"How was the ride?"

"Apparently Ambassador Bielke is not very interested in sheep. And we were not very fortunate with the weather," said Maggie, trying hard not to smile too broadly.

She turned to Bielke, who had begun to drip on the checkerboard marble floor.

"You should change. And I am sure Mrs Cook can help restore your jacket. You only need to ask her."

Bielke muttered what Maggie was sure was Swedish for "Humpf!" and trudged upstairs.

Thomas came up to Maggie and gave her a hug.

"Hang up your jacket. And then come find me. I think you're going to need my help doing something about your hair," he murmured.

Susan Alexander

Chapter 7

The von Fersens had also been unhappy with the weather and, having seen the Ashmolean and a couple of the older colleges, spent most of their remaining time in Oxford in the bar at the Randolph. However, any alcoholic glow had worn off by the time they returned and the entire crowd could only be described as cranky.

Maggie, who had her own glow from having had Thomas' help with her hair, decided to rise above the mood of her guests as they ate their dinner. As Bielke was sulking, she managed to draw out George Axel about his work as a judge and asked Elisabeth about her experiences teaching French. Maggie had her own repertoire of amusing anecdotes and, by the end of the meal, at least her end of the table was smiling, with the Ambassador being an exception.

After dinner, the older generation decided they would try billiards while the younger opted for bridge. Maggie watched the billiard players for a while, decided they were happy entertaining themselves, and went upstairs.

She peeked in the TV room and found Thomas sitting alone with a large whisky and watching the History channel. She sat down beside him and snuggled.

During a commercial break, he surprised her by asking, "How was your ride with Bielke?"

"You mean besides making Ned smile at his outfit? He failed to be captivated by our local flora and fauna. And he didn't seem to be particularly interested in sheep. I asked him if he had any anecdotes about sheep—he seems to have them about everything else and I understand Patagonia in Argentina where he was ambassador is full of flocks—and he said there were none he could tell in polite company. Fortunately it started to rain and we came back."

"I think he may be interested in something else we have at Beaumatin," said Thomas.

Maggie looked puzzled, then figured out what Thomas meant and shook her head.

"Elisabeth said he has been married three times. And can't afford to pay any more alimony. He's bored, or pretends to be, and amuses himself by… could you call it flirting?"

Thomas was watching her intently.

"But under all the polish and sophistication? I don't think he's a very nice man. Maybe that's why I find him unattractive. Plus he stinks from his cigarettes."

She sighed. "I suppose I should go back and be a good hostess."

Thomas played with one of the curls that had escaped her hairclip.

"It's Constance's party. Let her play hostess." And he kissed her.

Chapter 8

The next morning Maggie woke up in Thomas' bed. Thomas was up and getting dressed in riding clothes. He saw she was awake and kissed her.

"Going out with Ned?" she asked.

He nodded.

"Do you know what the plan is for our guests today?" he inquired.

"No idea. Perhaps Constance will organise a Christmas tree-trimming party. Did you see that tree? It's a monster. I thought Derek would start to cry when he thought about all the fairy lights he'd need to decorate it."

Thomas looked grim.

"It's only twelve more days. Or is it thirteen? Anyhow, I am sure time will march inexorably on like it always does and one morning we will wake up and find that both Swedes and fairy lights are gone," Maggie pointed out.

Thomas went off. Maggie realised she had forgotten to tell him about the unusual snowdrop she had seen. She thought. Freya and Loki, the Tibetan mastiffs Thomas had gotten to act as guard dogs and to discourage poachers, were at Ned's while there were so many houseguests. So if it really were a rare snowdrop, perhaps it would be better elsewhere. Just on GP--general principle.

Maggie got dressed, told Mrs Cook she would return for coffee shortly, and got a pot and a trowel from the greenhouse.

The snowdrop was still there, its outer segments still pin-striped in green.

She looked around but saw no one in the vicinity.

"This may be totally unnecessary," she told the snowdrop as she carefully dug it up and placed it in the pot. "But better to be safe than sorry. And until I find out if you have another name, I'm going to call you "Wolcom Yol." It means "Welcome Christmas" and Benjamin Britten wrote a beautiful song with that title."

Maggie returned to the kitchen and showed Mrs Cook the snowdrop.

"I'm not sure whether this is a special snowdrop or not. I need to ask Lord Raynham. But in the meantime I'm going to put it on the windowsill in my dressing room. Just to make sure it stays safe."

Mrs Cook nodded.

Maggie was on her third cup of coffee and answering emails in her study when Mrs Cook knocked and entered. The housekeeper was visibly upset.

"Lady Raynham? There's a problem."

"Oh dear. What now," Maggie wondered.

"Yes?"

"Do you remember that pair of Staffordshire china dogs? Those spaniels? Red and white? On one of the console tables in the drawing room? They're gone."

"Gone?"

"Yes. Gone. They're not there. Someone must have taken them."

Maggie tried to remember. She vaguely recalled the dogs. Strange looking. Almost primitive.

"I'm sure you're right. About their being gone. But let me go see."

They crossed the hall and went into the drawing room. Mrs Cook pointed. There was a space on a long, narrow table that backed a sofa.

"Oh dear."

The dogs were definitely gone.

"Could someone have knocked them off? Broken them? And cleaned up and been too embarrassed to admit what had happened?"

Mrs Cook considered this alternative scenario.

"Perhaps. But to break both dogs? The carpet should have provided some cushioning. And to have removed every last little shard? Besides, that's not all."

The housekeeper looked grim.

"Something else is missing?"

The housekeeper nodded.

"Two other things. From the library."

They went back across the hall and entered the room.

"A snuff box. From that case."

A display case held a collection of small antique items from various Barons Raynham. Seals. Spectacles. Scent bottles. Fobs. Letter openers. There was a space. No snuff box.

Maggie tried the lid. It lifted easily.

"It's never locked," said Mrs Cook.

"And then…" She led Maggie to another cabinet that held weapons—swords, rapiers and daggers.

"One of the daggers is missing as well. The one that was the third baron's, with the fancy gold handle that's inlaid with precious stones. It's extremely valuable." She pointed to a space.

"Oh dear. Let's go back to my study."

The two women looked at each other.

"Should I tell Lord Raynham?" Mrs Cook asked.

"No. Or at least not yet. He's unhappy enough about having so many guests in the house. Not to mention that reporter and his photographer."

Mrs Cook frowned at the mention of Trueblood-Fitch and Knowles, of whom she obviously disapproved.

Maggie made a mental list of all the people who were at Beaumatin.

"Well it's not you or me or Lord Raynham. Or Ned or any of the men. Or Damien or Derek. Or Mrs Griggs or Mrs Bateson."

Mrs Cook nodded in agreement.

"And it's not Constance. Or Nils."

Much as Maggie was not fond of Constance, she refused to believe she was involved. And her fiancé had visited several times without incident. In fact, Maggie quite liked Nils.

"That leaves the von Fersens. Is it possible one of them is a kleptomaniac?"

"And don't forget that Trueblood Fitch. And that Knowles. Calls himself a photographer." Mrs Cook was contemptuous.

Maggie thought.

"Can you talk to Mrs Griggs and Mrs Bateson? Perhaps when you or they are cleaning, they could keep a look out. Both in the guests' rooms and anyplace else someone could have concealed the dogs. And the snuff box. And the dagger."

Mrs Cook nodded.

"I know there are hundreds of places here where something could be hidden. But I can't think of a better plan. Can you? And it's not like we can accuse anyone. Even if we find the items. It would be terrible for Constance. And the wedding.

"And please, when you talk to Mrs Griggs and Mrs Bateson, make sure they know there's no question that we think they're involved."

Mrs Cook nodded again.

"And I'll keep an eye out as well."

Mrs Cook left. Maggie sighed. What more could go wrong?

In a moment she found out as Damien came in. He also looked upset.

"I hope I'm not disturbing you, but I couldn't stand it any longer."

"Of course not, Damien. What's the matter?"

"It's that man. That Trueblood-Fitch. He's... he's flirting with my Derek!"

"Trueblood-Fitch is flirting with Derek?"

"Yes. Damn him. It's as though I'm not even there."

"Really? And what do you mean, he's flirting?"

"Standing too close. Whispering things. And I saw him give Derek a pat on his cute little bum!"

"Oh dear. And what is Derek doing?"

"I think he's trying to be polite. Getting into *Country Style* would be great publicity. Derek rolled his eyes at me when he thought that piece of primordial slime couldn't see him. But still, Trueblood-Fitch must know we're a couple. How can he be so crass?"

"I'm afraid if his taste in tweed is any indication, crass is his style."

That got a smile from Damien.

"Do you think I'm over-reacting?"

"No. If he's doing what you say, it's understandable that you'd be upset. In fact, let's go see what Trueblood-Fitch is up to. Where are they?"

"Decorating the big tree. It's in the dining room."

Wolcum Yole

Maggie crossed the hall with Damien.

Calling the tree big was an understatement. It was ginormous, to use a term favoured by Maggie's niece Brooke. It reached the room's high ceiling and it would have taken more than three Maggie's joining hands to circle its circumference.

Derek was perched on a ladder hanging an elaborate ornament, a Renaissance angel wearing rich brocade robes and blowing on a trumpet. Other angels played lutes and violins and cymbals and horns and tambours. Fairy lights had already been distributed generously among the branches.

"How does it look?" Derek called down to Trueblood-Fitch, who was holding the ladder. Today the man was wearing a barleycorn tweed in orange, brown and purple. Maggie winced.

"Perfect. It's perfect," said the reporter. "Just like you, my dear boy."

"Yuck," thought Maggie, glancing at Damien.

Damien called, "Derek, it's Maggie. She's come to see the tree."

Trueblood-Fitch started. Derek turned.

"Hi Maggie!"

Derek climbed down the ladder.

"Thanks, Lionel. So Maggie. What do you think?"

"It's magnificent, Derek. Did you get costumes for us as well so when we're dining here we'll be coordinated? And a lutist?"

71

"That's not a bad idea. Don't you have any lutists in Oxford?"

"Probably several. But I suspect they're already booked for the season."

Derek looked disappointed.

Damien said, "There's just one thing left. The finial. Maggie, why don't you put it on?"

"Me?"

"Yes. It's your tree, after all. Climb up and I'll hand it to you."

"Um… You know I'm…"

"What? Are you scared of heights?"

"No. It's just… Oh, all right."

Maggie cautiously climbed up the ladder. Damien handed her the finial, a golden globe with a spike elaborately patterned with silver glitter.

Teetering a bit, Maggie managed to put the finial on, then began to climb back down the ladder. But her foot missed a step and she slipped and fell.

"Maggie!" cried Derek.

Strong arms caught her.

"Oh!"

It was Bielke. She could tell by the smell of his cigarettes even before she saw who it was.

"Oh dear. Sorry. Thank you."

He was still holding her.

"You can put me down now, please."

"And if I don't please," he murmured.

Thomas was standing in the doorway.

"Maggie? What's going on?"

Bielke set Maggie down.

"You know me. What a klutz I am. Damien asked me to put the finial on top of the tree and I slipped coming down the ladder. Fortunately, Ambassador Bielke caught me."

"Indeed."

Maggie came and put her arm through Thomas'. He was stiff. Frosty.

"Come admire the tree. Isn't it magnificent?"

Damien moved the ladder away from the tree.

"What do you think?" he asked.

"I told them we should hire a lutist to play while we eat. Assuming Constance hasn't thought of that already."

"Are you sure you have enough fairy lights?" was Thomas' comment.

Derek giggled.

Thomas looked at Maggie. His face was expressionless.

"One of the ewes had a mishap. Cyril Westcott, the vet, is coming to see if she can be saved. I came to tell you not to wait lunch."

"Oh dear. I'm so sorry. I hope it will be all right."

Thomas left.

Bielke came over.

"Are you sure you're all right?"

"Yes. I'm just clumsy, I'm afraid."

Maggie looked at her watch.

"Lunch in an hour. In the meantime, I have some work to do. So if you'll excuse me. And Damien, let's talk this afternoon."

Maggie retreated to her study.

Good grief. The snowdrop. The thefts. Bielke. Trueblood-Fitch. And now Thomas deciding to be frosty. Perhaps she should have booked that flight to Ulan Bator after all.

As that was not an option, she called Anne, but got her friend's voice mail. Then she remembered. Anne was in Devon visiting her husband Laurence's parents. Maggie was on her own.

Or perhaps not quite on her own. There was a knock on her door. It was Mrs Cook who announced that Lady Ainswick was there and was asking for Lady Raynham.

Lady Ainswick was in her mid-sixties. Of medium height and slight, she had blue eyes and wiry grey hair that was pulled back into a bun. Her face was devoid of makeup and still showed traces of the beautiful woman who had married the ninth Viscount Ainswick more than forty years before.

Wolcum Yole

"Maggie. I came to deliver a present for Constance." She indicated the large shopping bag she was carrying.

"Chloe said Constance wanted a wok. A wok? In my day we got candlesticks and chafing dishes and sterling soup ladles. But I guess times change."

"They do, don't they?"

Beatrix looked at Maggie shrewdly. "I also wanted to see how you are holding up. Gweneth said Constance has foisted ten members of Nil's family on you. I found that hard to believe."

"Unfortunately, it's true. I'm at the point where I wish I would be carried off by space aliens for experimentation. At least until after New Years' which is when I understand they will finally depart."

"That long? But the wedding's on the 22nd."

"I know. They'll be here for both Christmas and New Years'. And it would have been Thomas' and my first…"

"Really. That girl," said Beatrix in disgust.

"And I have a problem… I wonder if I could ask you for advice. Once again," Maggie smiled ruefully.

"Of course."

"It's one of Nils' family. His uncle. His mother's brother. He's been… flirting with me. Being inappropriate. Physically inappropriate. I don't want to be rude. Or cause any unpleasantness before the wedding. But Thomas has noticed and I get the feeling he may think I'm encouraging Bielke—that's his name. Franz Bielke. Ambassador Bielke. A distinguished diplomat. Retired. He has a reputation for being a ladies' man. He's been married three times. And I think what he's doing... it's because he's bored. Or is trying to cause trouble. I'm just not sure what to do."

"In my experience there's a Bielke at every wedding. Someone who's a problem. Unfortunately usually a family member which makes it hard to exclude them. Unless you elope.

"At my wedding it was my Uncle Albert. I had warned my bridesmaids to avoid being alone with him but he trapped poor Edwina when she was coming back from the ladies' cloak room. People heard her screaming and came running. It caused quite a scene." Beatrix shook her head at the memory.

"And now I must be going. There's always so much to do before the holidays. You're lucky to have Mrs Cook."

."I know," Maggie agreed.

"So keep a stiff upper lip and I'll see you on Saturday," said Beatrix.

She picked up the shopping bag. "A wok? Why would anyone want a wok? You certainly can't use one on an Aga."

The door closed and Maggie frowned. She was already keeping a stiff upper lip. And staying away from Uncle Albert for the duration of a wedding reception was not the same as having to live under the same roof for sixteen days with a... a predator.

Maggie decided she would just have make sure she kept Bielke at a distance. And certainly never be alone with him. No getting trapped coming back from the ladies' cloak room.

Chapter 9

Maggie sighed. Lunch was nearly over, Thomas was still out. The afternoon stretched ahead.

As far as Maggie knew, Constance had not planned any outing or activity. And the von Fersens did not seem inclined to entertain themselves.

When Maggie's friends from Oxford visited, they tended to bring laptops and tablets and smart phones as well as reading matter and, between reading and being connected and enjoying collegial banter, were a hostess' dream guests.

The von Fersens were the opposite case. Although she had seen that several of the younger generation had smart phones, no one had brought a laptop or tablet and it seemed they had not arranged for international roaming. Nor did they seem to be readers. They were indifferent to the extensive selection of recreational literature to be found in the guest rooms and, if the issue were a lack of fluency in English, had not packed any books in Swedish either. Or picked up some paperbacks at the airport before they left. The exception was Bielke, and Maggie suspected his request for a copy of her book was more about his ongoing flirtation with her than out of any genuine interest.

Why hadn't Constance organised a visit to London? With its museums and theatres and shops and Christmas lights. And both she and Nils had done their graduate work in epidemiology there, so it wasn't that they didn't know the city.

"Well, not my problem," Maggie tried to convince herself.

Except in some ways, it was her problem. Whatever she felt privately, Beaumatin was ostensibly her home. She was the hostess. It was her responsibility to see that her guests were comfortable and cared for. And if what Bielke said were true, Constance had already prejudiced the von Fersens against her. She did not want to confirm that impression.

Over coffee and tea, Constance announced that the younger members of the party had decided to go see a movie in Cheltenham. *The Hobbit* had opened. The older von Fersens were not enthusiastic and Maggie noted several glances her way.

Oh dear. It was raining, so proposing riding or shooting was not an option. Then she was rescued from an unexpected quarter.

"As the weather is so dreary, why don't we play bridge?" It was Bielke.

Georg Axel and Carl Magnus and Anna Sofia nodded enthusiastically. Pregnant Agneta said she would stay and play as well. Elisabeth assented with some resignation and even Ulrika agreed.

Bielke turned to his hostess.

"We need an eighth. Do you play?"

"Cards? Um. I played some bridge in graduate school. Not well compared to some. Certainly not competitively. And I never seem to have much luck with my cards."

Bielke smiled. "You must let me partner you. As I have excellent luck with cards."

Wolcum Yole

"Really? What is that saying? Lucky at cards, unlucky at love?" Maggie couldn't resist.

Bielke's ice blue eyes sparked. Then he leaned towards her and murmured, "That has certainly not been my experience."

Oh dear. Did he think she was flirting? She remembered what Elisabeth had said and glanced over at the woman, who was trying to keep her face expressionless and her attention elsewhere. Maggie wondered if perhaps she should try to talk to Elisabeth in private. She suspected she had more to tell her. And she supposed it was even possible that the woman had at some point in the past constituted some of Bielke's "luck."

The movie-goers left. With Mrs Cook's assistance, an additional card table was set up in the game room.

Was it too early for drinks? Mrs Cook had also set up a table with assorted beverages, from juice to whisky, and snacks. Maggie saw there was a bottle of white Burgundy in a cooler, open and tempting, but decided she would wait. She would need all her wits if she were not going to embarrass herself. The von Fersens might not read, but it seemed they were serious about cards.

Ulrika partnered Anna Sofia, opposite Carl Magnus and Agneta. Bielke insisted on playing with Maggie, leaving Georg Axel with Elisabeth.

Bielke was an aggressive bidder and won several hands, leaving a relieved Maggie to be the dummy and sit and watch. Which was fine with her. However, he seemed to lose nearly as often as he won and Maggie could see his rising irritation. She suspected he wanted to show off for her.

Then Maggie ended up winning an impossible bid, urged on by her partner. She had to play every card perfectly. A grand slam.

Bielke came with his unpleasant odour of stale smoke and stood behind her. He put his hand on her shoulder while he watched her play. Without being obvious he tightened his grip to indicate when he disapproved of her card choice and let it rest lightly when he agreed.

"He's cheating," Maggie thought. "Why am I not surprised?"

She thought of the Police song, *Don't Stand So Close to Me,* and wished the man would return to his side of the table. He did not, of course.

Maggie noticed Elisabeth glancing at them. She looked worried. Had Bielke been the same with her? Flirted? Been too familiar? Gone even further? She really had to talk to her.

Maggie had two cards left to play. Her intuition said to play one, but Bielke disagreed. To the point she was sure she would have bruises from where he was gripping her shoulder.

"Tough tuna, Bielke," she thought and played her own card choice.

It had been the right move.

Maggie was being congratulated by Elisabeth and Georg Axel and was getting a hug from Bielke.

"So you have a mind of your own," he was murmuring when Thomas came in.

He took in the scene and his face became expressionless.

"Oh dear," Maggie thought. She stood up so suddenly that Bielke was thrown off balance and staggered back.

Maggie crossed to Thomas. "I just won a hand. Apparently given my unimpressive level of skill, there was general rejoicing. How is the ewe?"

"She had to be put down," Thomas said coldly.

"Oh. I'm sorry." Maggie put her hand on his arm but he removed it.

"You seem to have our guests… entertained. I'll leave you to your amusements."

He turned and left.

Maggie endured another two hours of card play. Fortunately she did not win another bid. Drinks were served and the von Fersens became more cheerful and reverted to Swedish.

That was fine with Maggie, who felt sick at the thought that Thomas might have misunderstood what he had seen. Surely he didn't believe that she found Bielke attractive or that she was encouraging his attentions.

Maggie decided she would have to talk to Bielke and make her position clear. Even if it risked unpleasantness. Anything was preferable to having Thomas upset. And having him think…

Maggie attention was recalled by Bielke, who reminded her that she needed to bid.

The movie goers returned and the card players suspended their games.

"We'll make a bridge player of you yet," said Georg Axel cheerfully.

Maggie smiled politely.

Maggie saw Elisabeth heading for the stairs and followed her.

"Elisabeth?"

"Yes?" the woman was cautious.

"I wondered. If you had a moment? Could we…"

Maggie was interrupted by the appearance of Bielke.

He saw the two women and came over.

"Elisabeth?" He pulled her aside and spoke softly and rapidly in Swedish. Elisabeth turned pale. Bielke continued. Elisabeth nodded and spoke softly in return.

Bielke turned to Maggie.

"Sorry to have interrupted. Carl Magnus can't find something he thinks is important," Bielke smirked and walked off.

"I'm sorry. Carl Magnus…" Elisabeth gestured and then fled up the stairs, leaving Maggie standing alone.

"What in the world was that about," she wondered.

Maggie had retreated to her study and was pondering her predicament when Damien came in.

"Hi, Maggie. Am I interrupting?"

"No. No, that's all right."

"I just couldn't stand it any longer."

"Trueblood-Fitch?"

"Yes. His onslaught continues."

"Oh dear."

"I know Derek would never... Well, certainly not with someone like Trueblood-Fitch. But still. And he's so blatant about it. It's like I'm not there."

Maggie immediately empathised. Bielke was doing the same thing to her.

"Would you like me to talk to Trueblood-Fitch?"

Damien thought about this.

"What you would tell him?"

"To stop. Leave you—both of you—alone. You have work to do. He's disturbing it. Upsetting the household. Worst case I can threaten to complain to his editor. It's amazing—to me at least—that being Lady Raynham of Beaumatin can get you the immediate attention of quite a few people. Especially editors of high-end magazines."

"You'd do that?"

"Of course."

Damien looked conflicted.

"Well. Thank you. That's really nice of you. Let me think about it. It would still be great to get into *County Style*."

"I understand. Let me know if you want me to talk to him. Otherwise, I'm here if you just need to come in and, er, let off steam."

They hugged and Damien returned to decorating the ballroom.

Maggie thought about the offer she had made Damien and then decided that she should see if someone would do the same for her. Like Thomas. She went to find her husband.

Maggie knocked on Thomas' study door and entered. He was sitting at his desk and working at his laptop, which had been a birthday present from Maggie.

"Thomas?"

"Yes?" he scowled.

Oh dear. Thomas was definitely in Sub Zero mode.

"Um, are you busy?"

"Yes," he snapped.

"Oh. I'm sorry. But I wondered… If you had a moment. I have a problem…"

"I told you I was busy."

"Yes, but…"

"No. Just… go."

"Thomas…"

Thomas tensed and looked like he was about to get up and forcibly eject her from the room.

Maggie looked stricken. She turned and fled.

Thomas saw Maggie's expression, the one she got when he had hurt her. Well, he didn't care. If she thought she could humiliate him while she carried on with that smarmy Swede and then come to him….

He went back to filling in the government form detailing the death of the ewe.

Constance had organised dinner at a local pub with a good kitchen, followed by its quiz night. Maggie, who was usually a highly-valued contributor to any team, was not invited to join.

"Whatever," she told herself. At least the house would be von Fersen-free for an evening.

Maggie went to see Mrs Cook. Lord Raynham, it seemed, had told her he had work to do and had requested a sandwich. That Trueblood-Fitch had gone along to the pub with the others. She didn't know where that photographer person was.

Maggie thanked the housekeeper and told her she wasn't hungry. Which was true. The idea that Thomas was avoiding her made her feel too sick to want to eat.

She decided she would go lick her wounds in her study. On the way she remembered the bottle of white Burgundy that had been open in the game room. Was it possible that it was still there?

It was still there. She took the bottle in its cooler and a glass with her. The Global Press, her publishing house, had sent her a half dozen advance copies of her new book that would come out in January. She was curious to re-read what she'd written.

She also decided she would play some Christmas music. Maggie loved Christmas. The lights. The bustle. The seasonal cheer. But most of all the carols. She knew the words to nearly all of them by heart and, if she were sure that no one was listening, would sing along when she could.

"Mormon Tabernacle Choir, bring it on!" she said.

Maggie was curled up on her sofa reading and beginning a third glass of wine. Both the wine and the book were good, she decided.

The study door opened. She hoped it was Thomas, but it was Bielke.

"Am I disturbing you? May I come in?"

"Yes. No. I mean, yes you are disturbing me, so no, please don't come in." Maggie stated emphatically.

Bielke looked surprised. He began to back out.

"No. Wait." She stood up.

He raised his eyebrows.

"I need to… I want to tell you…"

Maggie was flustered. She had never had to say something like this to anyone before.

Now Bielke was interested. He stepped back in.

"Yes?"

Maggie took a deep breath.

"I feel you are being inappropriate. In your behaviour. To me. And I'd appreciate it if you'd stop."

There. She'd said it. Not very articulately, but he'd have to know what she meant.

Bielke's eyes narrowed.

"You feel my behaviour is inappropriate?"

"Yes. You're being too… physical."

"But I find most women enjoy it when I am, as you say, physical."

"Well I'm not. Most women. And I don't. Care for it."

"Ah. I see. This is your idea of playing hard to get."

Maggie recoiled.

"I am not playing… I told you. I don't like it. I really don't like it. And it's causing problems for me."

"Problems between you and your priggish husband?"

"He's not… Yes. Between Thomas and me."

"I see."

"Good. I'm glad you do."

"But what if I want to cause problems? Between you and your stuffy baron. Then my behaviour is perfectly appropriate."

Maggie stared at him in dismay.

"You can't…"

"Oh no? Why not?"

"Please…"

"Just watch me," he taunted.

Maggie was suudenly so angry, she hurled the glass of wine she was holding at Bielke's head. It hit the door frame and shattered. Wine splattered and pieces of crystal stuck to his black suit jacket.

Bielke laughed. He took out a pocket handkerchief and flicked off bits of glass.

"You know, I am going to enjoy this. And I wasn't sure I could enjoy anything anymore."

He went out and closed the door behind him.

Maggie stared at the door in dismay. She had never, ever, thrown anything. At anyone. What had she been thinking?

Well, the point was, she hadn't been thinking. She was glad she hadn't had a gun, because there was no doubt that she would have shot Bielke. And there would have been no justification of self-defence. Well, none within the legal definition.

She went to the kitchen and got a dust pan and brush to clean up the glass. She swept up the shards, then went to the library and got another glass. Back in her study, she filled it with the Burgundy and continued reading to take her mind off her problems.

Later, Maggie was getting ready for bed when there was a soft knocking on her door.

She opened it to Thomas,

"Oh. Thomas. I'm so glad. I really need to…"

Wolcum Yole

"I didn't come here to talk," he said and locked the door.

Susan Alexander

Chapter 10

It was the day before the wedding. Maggie was in what she knew as Beaumatin's music room, but which seemed to have been turned into a ballroom. Derek and Damien had put up clouds of white tulle that lowered the high ceiling and had distributed more fairy lights throughout the fabric so that they twinkled like stars. The walls were lined with tree branches that were sprayed white and sparkled with glitter.

To Maggie, it felt less like a Winter Wonderland and more like C. S. Lewis' Narnia where, in thrall to the White Witch, "it was always Winter, and never Christmas."

Maggie knew the following evening she'd be expected to dance. With Thomas. With Georg Axel von Fersen. With Nils and his other male relatives. With William. With James. With Lord Ainswick and Sir John Nesbitt and Simon Peevey and any other guest who asked her. Gweneth had prepped her on the protocol.

But remembering the protocol was the least of her worries. Maggie was not a good dancer. At least when it came to ballroom dancing. Give her the Stones or Madonna or even Lady Gaga and she was fine. But otherwise she was hopeless at following her partner's lead.

She had barely made it through the party following the wedding of the Ainswicks' daughter, Chloe, and that had been after hours of Thomas' patient tutelage. With the demands of her return to Oxford and her book tour, no additional practice had been possible. Or perhaps Thomas just thought that she was "cured" and would be fine for Constance's event.

But Constance had planned a ball in the classic sense of the term. Men were wearing white tie and tails and the women formal gowns. In fact, Maggie had spent more than she usually would on clothes for a year on a dress so spectacular she hoped no one would notice how badly she was doing the fox trot.

And she had to admit she was looking forward to seeing Thomas in his formal wear. He had looked so amazing the few times she had seen him in a tuxedo, she just hoped she didn't simply melt into a large puddle on the floor at the mere sight of him in tails.

Meanwhile, she had decided that, the same way baseball players visualise a home run before they swing at a pitch and long jumpers mentally rehearse their jumps, she would practice dancing in her mind. If the technique worked for Olympic high divers, why not for her?

And even though the burnt orange wool knit dress she was wearing, along with the impressive strands of the Raynham pearls, would not provide the same sensation as the full, sweeping skirt of her dress, well, she would imagine that too.

Maggie closed her eyes, put one hand up on an imaginary shoulder, and another as if it were being held up by her partner's hand. She was humming "Blue Moon," which she knew was one of Thomas' favourites, and remembering what it felt like to be in his arms, when suddenly she was embraced by an actual partner.

She opened her eyes expecting to see Thomas, but it was Franz Bielke.

"Charming," he said.

"Oh." Maggie halted abruptly.

Wolcum Yole

"No. Don't stop."

She tried to pull away, but Bielke held her tightly and whirled her across the floor until she was backed against a wall. As usual, he smelled unpleasantly of stale tobacco.

"I've waited for a moment like this for days," he said.

"No!" She raised her hand to push him back but he caught it, pressed against her and kissed her full on the lips.

Thomas had been looking for Maggie. He found her in the last place he would have expected. He came into the ballroom just in time to see Bielke lean into his wife and kiss her.

He was so shocked and angry he missed details such as Maggie's protest and her struggle to avoid the Swede. He strode over, grabbed the man and let fly a punch. It connected and Bielke went down.

Without stopping to see what he'd done, Thomas grabbed Maggie and dragged her into his study. He was breathing hard and clenching and unclenching his fists.

"God, Thomas. Thank you."

"What?"

"What an awful man!"

"You expect me to believe you had no part in that…in that..."

"What? No. Of course not. What do you think?"

"I think you've been flirting with Bielke for days. Encouraging him."

"I have not!"

"I've watched you."

"Then you misunderstood what you saw. I've felt obliged to be polite to a guest and when I tried to tell you…"

"I don't believe you."

"But…"

"Remember you talked about the three strikes rule? Well now I'm invoking it. The Christmas tree. The card game. Now this. Three strikes. You're out. I won't have Constance's wedding ruined by your shameless behaviour, so I expect you to play your part. But after that, it's over. We're finished."

"What?"

"You heard me."

Maggie couldn't believe what Thomas was saying. What was wrong with the man? Apparently there was no reasoning with him. She needed to let him calm down.

She turned to go.

"No. Wait."

She paused hopefully, but with one hand Thomas grabbed her arm and with the other he yanked on the strands of pearls around her neck.

"The Raynham jewels are not to be worn by a slut."

The string broke and pearls flew all over. The ornate gold clasp that joined them scratched the side of her neck and made a deep gash.

Wolcum Yole

"Ow!" She put her hand to her neck and her fingers came away covered in blood.

Maggie looked at Thomas in horror. She jerked arm away and darted from the room.

On her way to her bedroom for some first aid, Maggie's left and right brains weighed in.

Left brain: See. We told you. He's throwing us out again.

Right brain: No, he's not.

L.B.: Oh really? How else would you understand, "We're finished?"

R.B.: It's like before. He's misunderstood. He'll calm down and realise he made a mistake. And tell us he acted like an idiot. Again.

L.B.: Calm down when? Bielke's here for twelve more days.

R.B.: Twelve? That many? Are you sure?

L.B.: Yes. We're the one that's good at maths, remember?

Maggie was fortunate. Constance had arranged a visit to Bath for Nils' family and her friends from Geneva, so she was spared having to appear at lunch. It took her a long time to stop the bleeding. Thank goodness her outfit for the wedding and, more importantly, her ball gown were cut so they would hide the ugly wound.

As for Thomas, Maggie could only hope that his irrational behaviour was due to the stress of the wedding and the house being filled with so many guests and that he would calm down when the fairy lights had been taken down and everyone had left. And as for Bielke, she would keep her distance and make sure they were never alone together again.

Maggie may have been able to skip lunch, but she was unable to avoid dinner. Nils' family had organised a seasonal meal of Swedish specialties featuring many types of herring, meatballs, ham, gravlax, tiny sausages, potatoes, red cabbage and beets, washed down with various sorts of aquavit.

Maggie dreaded having to face Bielke, but he seemed unconcerned by what had happened, although his face was slightly puffy and he drank more than he ate.

In fact, when he pulled out Maggie's chair, he cast a triumphant look down to Thomas' end of the table. Maggie risked a glance and noticed Thomas' jaw was clenched and his brows were drawn together, but otherwise, with so many people between them, there was no chance for another altercation.

As the hostess, Maggie was required to drink quite a few glasses of aquavit, even though she did not like the harsh spirit. Since she was too upset to have an appetite, she soon felt quite ill and somewhat tipsy. She would need to be careful when she stood up.

Fortunately, both Constance and Nils were being taken out separately by their friends and dinner broke up early. Maggie managed get to the kitchen and up the back stairs and to her room without meeting Thomas or, more importantly, the ambassador. And if the older von Fersens needed entertaining, Thomas could play host. For once.

She locked her door, rushed into the bathroom and was sick. Her eyes teared. What a nightmare. She took two aspirin, drank a lot of water, set her alarm and crawled into bed.

Chapter 11

The day of the wedding was rainy and windy. Poor Constance, Maggie thought as she dressed. Even snow would have been better. As long as it wasn't so much it prevented people from getting to the church.

Maggie had bought a chic little midnight blue suit for her book launch and that was what she was wearing. Since she figured using any of the Raynham family jewellery would be the equivalent of waving a red flag at a bull as far as Thomas was concerned, she put on her own gold earrings and a dark blue felt cloche. And gloves. Gweneth had told her that gloves were a requirement. Not leather, not Thermalite, but cloth.

She was going to the church with Nils' parents. Thomas would go with Constance and Nils with his brother. As the "step-mother-of-the-bride," she would be seated in the front next to Thomas, but would not be the last person seated before the entrance of the bride, as would be the case if she were the actual MOB.

William escorted her to her seat, which was next to Gweneth and their son, Harry, followed by Victoria and her boys, Thomas and John. Young Elizabeth Conyers was serving as a flower girl and James was one of the ushers. The church was full. Maggie had once speculated about Gloucestershire social circles and now here they all were. Including the royals.

The sanctuary had been decorated for Christmas by Derek and Damien and smelled pleasantly of pine. A brass quintet had joined the organ in the choir loft and played Christmas music.

Maggie thought back to her own wedding which had been in the same sanctuary just seven months earlier. Hers had been as simple as Constance's was elaborate. Not even four pews had been filled. Did she regret that? Certainly not the event. The marriage might be another issue.

She hadn't seen Thomas since she had left the table the night before. She hoped he had calmed down. Well she would soon find out. The musicians had launched into Handel's *Water Music*, the Raynham equivalent of the Wagnerian *Here Comes the Bride*.

As expected, Constance looked lovely and radiant, in a white satin wedding dress heavily embroidered with pearls and a long train. Thomas was distinguished, Nils nervous but happy. When the time came for Thomas to step aside, Maggie noticed him glance at her, but she kept her gaze fixed firmly on the vicar. Thomas sat down next to her and did not pull away when their arms touched.

That was a good sign, she thought. Or maybe not. He had to be remembering their own wedding. Did he regret it? She risked a quick glance. His face was impassive.

Vows were exchanged, the bride was kissed and the musicians launched into more Handel.

The rain had paused long enough for there to be a receiving line outside. Maggie stood next to Thomas and remembered her instructions from Gweneth. She curtseyed when the royals were introduced and managed not to totter. The Duchess recognised her from one of her television interviews and congratulated her on her handling of "that dreadful little man." She said she wanted to read her book and Maggie promised to send her a copy. Thomas witnessed the exchange and could only nod when the Duchess told him how proud he should be of his accomplished wife before she moved on.

Wolcum Yole

The receiving line seemed endless. Some people Maggie knew, like the Ainswicks and the Nesbitts, but most she did not. She was also aware that she was the object of some curiosity as the second wife of the 28th Baron Raynham.

Maggie followed the rules of receiving lines. Make eye contact, smile, shake hands, unless one should curtsy, offer an appropriate remark or create an opening for the other person to say something.

When it began to rain again, the wedding party returned to Beaumatin, where Lionel Trueblood-Fitch organised people and the ferret-like Knowles took pictures in the great hall. After the few shots that required Maggie and Thomas were taken, she shut herself in her study until lunch. It was a slow email day, with most of the world in the countdown to Christmas. At least in her world, she reminded herself.

She glanced at her hands, ungloved, and noticed in her avoidance of anything linking "Raynham" and "jewellery" she had neglected to put on her wedding ring. Oh well. If Thomas had a problem with that, tough tuna.

Lunch was traditional. Cold meats and salads. Champagne. A cake. The newlyweds' friends from Sweden, England and Geneva had joined the families for the occasion, so the food was laid out on the dining room table as a buffet.

Maggie drank champagne and mostly skipped the rest. Toasts were made. To Maggie's surprise, Thomas' was somewhat strained and inarticulate. William's was eloquent and James' was quite funny. Fredrik's was in Swedish but, as the von Fersens were laughing, she assumed it was funny as well.

After the lunch, Maggie fled to her room. Too much champagne. And the rainy weather had been chilling. She needed water. She needed some more aspirin. She needed a nap. What she didn't need was to be disturbed by... anyone. She locked her door.

When she woke up, it was dark. She would get some coffee from Mrs Cook, shower and start to get ready for the ball.

While Maggie was in the shower, Bielke came and tapped softly on her door. There was no answer. He tapped again. Nothing. He tried the handle. Locked. He was turning away when he heard a noise.

Thomas was standing a few yards away. He was stiff and white with fury.

Bielke stared back. Then slowly, he smiled. If that pompous baron wanted to think he had caught him leaving his wife's bedroom, then let him. He could use the misunderstanding to his advantage.

Bielke turned and almost collided with Lionel Trueblood-Fitch. Stupid man. He swore in Swedish and stalked off. He did not look back.

Chapter 12

Ignorant of the scene that had occurred outside her door, Maggie was ready. Or as ready as she would ever be. The nap and aspirin and caffeine had done their work. She was polished and fragrant and subtly but skilfully made up. She took a deep breath and prepared to make an entrance.

She stopped on the landing of the grand stairway and peered over. Anna Sofia von Fersen stood below, talking to Thomas.

Oh my.

As she had expected, Thomas in his white tie and tails was magnificent. He was tall and thin, haughty perhaps, but his coat fit him perfectly and he seemed completely at ease in the clothing. Maggie felt strange, then realised she had been forgetting to breathe.

Thomas saw a movement out of the corner of his eye and looked up. Maggie was coming down the stairs. At least it seemed to be Maggie. It could also have been an elfish queen from one of Tolkien's fantasies. He was so bemused he forgot the murderous rage he was feeling at her betrayal for a moment.

In that moment he saw her pale, slender and seemingly nude except for delicate green twining vines that wove around her neck, down her arms, down her bodice, down her back, down her thighs. Then he realised they were embroidered onto flesh-toned fabric that fit her like a second skin to her hips, where the tulle flared out into a full skirt that trailed.

She looked amazing. Her hair was caught up by a golden clip shaped like a butterfly. That and the emerald and diamond wedding band Thomas had given her were the only jewels she wore.

Maggie smiled tentatively at Thomas. He felt a sick feeling in the pit of his stomach. Was she wearing that dress for him or that insufferable Swede? He stared back coldly in return.

Oh dear. Thomas was still in Ice Man mode. Sub Zero and heading lower.

Anna Sofia was exclaiming over her dress. Maggie smiled mechanically.

There was another receiving line. The bride, groom and parents, including Maggie. Most of the people who had been at the church were welcomed, passed into the ballroom and were offered champagne by waiters in Christmas-red jackets.

Gweneth had briefed Maggie well. The small orchestra began to play the first dance. The bride and groom led, then were followed by the bride's parents and the groom's. Thomas led her onto the dance floor, still an icicle.

As he took her in his arms and swept her into the dance, she told herself, "Maggie Eliot, you are not a lesser woman. Even though your husband is being a consummate idiot, you are going to behave with grace and dignity and live up to your dress and not let anyone know your heart is breaking."

So Maggie danced with Thomas and Georg Axel von Fersen and all the other von Fersen males and William and James and Lord Ainswick and Sir John Nesbitt and Simon Peevey and men whose names she couldn't remember. During breaks she was returned by her partner to Thomas' side.

Wolcum Yole

Then Franz Bielke approached. A stiff Thomas became a petrified Thomas. Bielke ignored his host, bowed to Maggie and asked her to dance.

Maggie glanced at Thomas, half hoping he would intervene, but got no reaction. Reluctant to cause a scene, she let Bielke lead her onto the dance floor.

Of course Bielke would be an excellent dancer. And he looked almost as splendid as Thomas in his tails, which he wore with a striped ribbon across his chest and a scattering of medals on his coat. She would have been impressed if she had not despised him. And if he still did not carry an unpleasant aroma of stale cigarette smoke.

As he whirled her around in a waltz, he murmured, "I have hardly been able to take my eyes off you the entire evening."

"That must have been agreeable for your other partners," responded Maggie tartly.

Bielke looked surprised.

"So she has claws," he commented.

Maggie decided to channel Thomas and look aloof.

"I tried to visit you earlier, you know. A pity your door was locked."

Maggie recoiled and tried to pull away but Bielke only tightened his grip.

"Perhaps the next time it will be open."

"If you even try to enter my room, I will shoot you. And you know I am a good shot."

"You have already shot Cupid's arrow straight into my heart. Isn't that enough for you?"

Maggie looked at Bielke in disgust.

"All right. We're done. Please take me back."

"I don't think so. And you don't want to cause a scene. Especially as your husband is watching us so intently. You don't want to give him the impression we're having a lover's quarrel, do you?"

Maggie was horrified and let it show.

Bielke smiled.

When the dance finally ended, Bielke walked her back to where Thomas was standing, his face expressionless.

Bielke bowed, smirked, walked off.

"Thomas?" Maggie put her hand on his arm, asking for... what? She wasn't sure.

"Come." He grasped her arm and walked her onto the floor. The orchestra was starting to play another waltz. Maggie knew it.

"Dmitri Shostakovich. Waltz No. 2," she said.

Thomas raised his brows.

"Shostakovich, Waltz No. 2," she repeated. It had hints of the circus. And gypsies. It was beautiful. Poignant. Haunting.

Thomas swept her into the dance. She nearly stumbled.

Wolcum Yole

"What is he doing? He knows I can't dance like this," Maggie thought in a panic.

Was he trying to humiliate her? Because he felt humiliated by Bielke?

Thomas changed course without warning and she nearly tripped.

All right. Now she was angry. She hadn't done anything wrong. And she could do this. She had to. She let her mind go blank except for the music and focussed on Thomas' right ear, turning it into an abstract sculpture.

Thomas felt Maggie withdraw and go off someplace deep inside her head. Eliotshire, he called it. But she was dancing. Surprisingly well. He whirled her around to the music, her skirt billowing behind her. She had never been able to follow him like this before. What had changed?

Thomas danced with Maggie twice more and she used what she decided to call the "out of body" technique to make it through. It may not have made her an interesting partner, but at least she no longer stepped on Thomas' toes.

A midnight buffet had been set up in the dining room of foie gras, smoked salmon, seafood in tiered metal stands, ham sliced paper thin, small pastries. Waiters circulated with hors d'oeuvres and champagne. Its acidity upset Maggie's stomach. She wished she could have some of Thomas' white Burgundy but knew she couldn't ask.

There was a final receiving line. Maggie endured it. She smiled and offered Christmas wishes. As soon as the last guest had left, she fled to her room.

Susan Alexander

Chapter 13

Maggie was exhausted. Her stomach was upset from the champagne. She just stood, too tired to struggle out of her dress. Her wonderful dress which she had hoped would work magic, but had failed. What was that term from Harry Potter? She was a squib.

Maggie heard a noise and was horrified to see the doorknob turning. She had forgotten to lock the door. She was afraid it would be Bielke. And she had no gun with which to shoot him as she had threatened.

But it was Thomas. Still in his white tie and tails. Still looking magnificent if somewhat tired.

Thomas had been drinking whisky heavily. While not completely drunk, he was very far from sober. He saw Maggie, half obscured behind a bedpost. That outrageous bed. With its carved pagoda roof and gilded dragons rampant. And that dress.

She had turned from being an elfish queen into an exotic forest creature. Wary. Poised for flight. He turned and locked the door and pocketed the key. Flight was no longer an option.

Was she false? Part of him doubted and part believed. He had seen the flirtation, the kiss, that damnable Bielke walking away from her door. Was she false?

"Come here."

Maggie gave the faintest shake of her head. Thomas was no longer icy. What was he, then? She didn't recognise his mood. But it made her cautious.

He crossed to her. He turned her and gently removed her hair clip so her curls tumbled loose. He tossed the clip into a corner.

Was she false? He decided not to think about that for the moment.

"Thomas? Wait. Please…"

He ignored her.

Chapter 14

Maggie woke up. She was alone. From the light she guessed it was late. Nine o'clock at least. People would be up and having breakfast and expecting their hostess.

She was still exhausted. Thomas had not let her have enough sleep.

Aspirin. A long hot shower for her aching muscles and… other places. And caffeine. A lot of caffeine.

Maggie put her legs over the side of the bed and onto the floor. No, not the floor. They had landed on cloth. She looked down. It was her dress. Or what was left of it.

She picked it up. Fabric was torn. Ripped. Stained. Ruined. She let it fall back onto the floor. Whatever had happened last night, it had been more about venting anger than making love.

She spent a long time in the shower. Until the aspirin started to work and some of the soreness left. She emerged, towel-drying her hair.

Bielke was sitting in one of the chairs by the window.

"I've been admiring your room."

He gestured to the Chinese bed. And the large, gilt-framed mirror that leaned against one wall.

"Hardly the room of a staid professor. Or the wife of some rustic baron. More like a courtesan…"

He stood.

"Come one step closer and I'll scream," she threatened.

He raised his hands in a placating gesture.

"You're in no danger. I never try to seduce a woman when I'm... hung over."

He sat back down.

"And from the looks of things, you have already had a bit of a night."

He indicated the tangle of bed linens, her dress lying on the floor and Thomas' jacket which had been tossed onto the chair next to his. He smiled unpleasantly. Maggie flushed.

"And there's no one around to hear you screaming anyway. Everyone has gone off to explore some of your quaint villages and your husband has ridden out with... Is it Fred? Or Ted?"

"It's Ned. But that doesn't matter. You must leave."

"I don't think so. We need to talk."

"I have nothing to say to you."

"But I think you will find I have something to say to you. And you would do well to listen."

Maggie hesitated. She was wearing a short, silky, sea green nightgown that left little to the imagination. From his expression, Bielke was finding it interesting, despite what he'd said about a hangover.

She shrugged.

"I need to dress."

"Too bad. But I'll wait." Bielke leered.

Maggie grabbed some clothes from her closet and locked herself in the bathroom. She came out in moments in a bulky sweater and pants.

"So?" She stood defiantly, her arms folded across her chest.

Bielke crossed one long leg over the other and steepled his fingers. He had the look of a man who was about to enjoy himself.

"Although I have a generous pension from having been a member of our illustrious foreign service, I have discovered it is not enough. Taxes are high. I have ex-wives who want money. And one must keep up appearances.

"So I have found a side line which is useful in generating… supplementary income, shall we say. I have become a dealer in information. I buy. I sell…"

"You're a spy?"

"Oh no. My information tends to be of a more personal nature."

Maggie was puzzled. And failed to see what any of this had to do with her.

"People pay me to keep things… private."

Maggie suddenly understood.

"You're a blackmailer."

"That's such an ugly term. I prefer to think of myself as performing a sort of social arbitrage."

Nils' uncle was a blackmailer. A petty criminal. She wondered what his family would think. With their condescension and assumption of superiority.

"And what does this have to do with me?" Maggie demanded.

"Ah. That's the question, isn't it?" Bielke smiled smugly.

"Well?"

Last night, you may remember…"

Bielke paused, got up, walked over, and picked Maggie's dress up from off the floor. He saw its tattered state and shook his head.

"Pity. So perhaps you have more, er, interesting things to remember. At any event, while we were dancing, I mentioned that I had tried to pay you a visit yesterday. But found your door was locked."

"Yes. And I remember, quite clearly, that I said I would shoot you if you tried that again."

"But you haven't shot me."

"Only because I have not yet had a chance to visit the gun room."

"And we digress. What I did not tell you was that your husband saw me at your door. And I'm afraid he may have gotten the wrong impression."

Maggie froze.

"What do you mean, the wrong impression?"

"I'm afraid he may have thought he had found me coming out of your room."

"What?"

"And it suited me not to correct his misapprehension."

Maggie was afraid she was going to be sick. Oh God. No wonder Thomas had been so furious.

"He does tend towards jealousy, does he not? Which I find strange, since you so obviously adore him. These British aristocrats. They can be quite thick. So reserved. So stuffy. Although perhaps not always stuffy." Bielke nodded towards her dress.

"Anyhow. Down to business. I would be happy to disabuse your husband of his misapprehensions about my visit and the, er, nature of our relationship for a mere £20,000."

Maggie was speechless.

"Surely it would be worth that much to you."

She glared at him.

"Otherwise, I fear I will continue my pursuit of you and give everyone the impression we are in the middle of a torrid affair. And that any hostility on your part is just an attempt to cover it up. You marriage won't last until New Year's."

Maggie went white. If he did as he threatened her marriage wouldn't last through Christmas. Thomas had already said it was finished and that was before he had found Bielke at her door.

115

Bielke misinterpreted her look.

"Of course, I know how poorly you professors are compensated. And I would assume Raynham keeps you on a tight leash, financially speaking. Perhaps in other ways as well."

He glanced at the dress again and smiled.

"If £20,000 is too much at one go, I am sure we could work out a payment plan. Or there are the Raynham jewels. I understand the diamonds are quite spectacular and I know a jeweller who could easily substitute fakes for the genuine stones."

Maggie just stared at him.

Then Bielke saw something else that caught his interest. He walked over, squatted down and examined a lacy corset, matching garter belt and lace-topped stockings that had also ended up on the floor. His expression changed and he approached her.

"Or we could say £10,000 and work out other ways for you to pay off the remaining balance."

He suddenly turned and grabbed her.

"Ugh. No!"

He stank of stale smoke and whisky.

He forced her back onto the bed.

"No! You're hurting me!"

He caught her arms.

"Ow. Stop!"

When he tried to kiss her, Maggie brought her knee up between his legs. It was not a direct hit. Bielke did not fall writhing to the floor, but he did release her to bend over and clutch himself.

Maggie sprang up, grasped the back of his shirt and forced him towards the door.

She yanked it open.

"Get out. Just get out. And go to hell!"

Bielke managed to stand upright and pulled his jacket back in place. Outside, in the hall, he paused.

"You're upset. You need some time to consider. And would it really be so bad? Other women have found me…"

Maggie slammed the door in his face before he could finish and locked it.

"Oh my god. What am I going to do?" she wondered.

Susan Alexander

Chapter 15

Maggie went in search of some desperately needed coffee. If she were going to figure a way out of this mess, she needed caffeine. A lot of caffeine.

The von Fersens were back. The rain had been too much to make strolling through Tetbury enjoyable, although several of them carried bags indicating the inclement weather had not prevented them from shopping.

Anna Sofia compared the British weather unfavourably with Sweden's, while Georg Axel complained about the dimness of the light.

"At least we have snow to brighten things up during the darkest days. Right, Carl Magnus?"

Maggie felt like she needed to get away from all this. Wasn't it Sartre who'd written, "Hell is other people?" He'd been right about that.

She'd go outside for a bit. After more than eight years in England, she was immune to the rain and if her curls went into overdrive, it didn't matter. It was only the von Fersens and Thomas' family today.

Maggie was heading towards the mud room when she paused, then detoured. She went into the gun room and removed the smallest of the hand guns, a .22. She loaded it and slipped it into her pants pocket.

Let Bielke try to touch her. Or even come too close. Just let him try. She was prepared.

Maggie returned to the mud room and pulled on a jacket and some boots. With all the other work she was undertaking, Mrs Cook didn't need people treading dirt into the house,

Maggie walked around in the gardens. She was still in a state from Bielke's visit, in fact from all the things that had been going on in the days leading up to it. When she was far enough away from the house, she took out the gun and fired a few times at a plane tree, imagining it was her Swedish persecutor.

That felt better. She tried to breathe deeply and achieve some calm. She could see green shoots from the snowdrops coming up everywhere. And some hellebores that were well along. Tiny cyclamen leaves were also appearing. And other bits of green. Winter had barely started and here were signs that spring would follow. She should find comfort in that. And hope.

Maggie found herself in one of the gardens farthest from the house. Where the early snowdrops were blooming and she had seen the unusual snowdrop. She stopped short.

Franz Bielke was lying on the path. His ice blue eyes were open but unseeing. There was blood everywhere. Where his throat had been there was now just torn flesh. And a garden trowel had been driven deep into his chest.

Maggie swallowed and told herself she was not going to be sick. She wondered for a brief moment if one of her shots had accidentally hit him. But no, his wounds were definitely from the trowel. She knelt down beside the body and felt for a pulse. Nothing. Not a surprise. A faint smell of cigarette smoke lingered. She absently wiped her bloody fingers on her jacket. What should she do?

Maggie was experiencing a range of feelings. Revulsion at the act itself. Relief that she would no longer be the object of Bielke's harassment. Elation at the downfall of a man she considered to be an enemy. And even as she rebuked herself for having that feeling, she rationalised. Bielke had been an evil man and she was certain he had not been an innocent victim here.

Had he been blackmailing someone else? She had threatened to shoot the man. And feeling the way she did about him, it had not been an idle threat. Perhaps whoever had done this had felt the same way and used whatever means had been at hand.

She checked and was relieved that she had her mobile in her other pants pocket. And was getting a signal. Not all parts of the grounds had reception.

First she'd call William. Then she'd call Willis, the police detective inspector she knew. Then she'd find Thomas. He could decide how to handle the von Fersen family. And the others.

William was home and, from the noise in the background, was playing with his children.

"William. It's Maggie. I'm afraid… It's not good."

"What's not good, Maggie?" William sounded concerned and Maggie heard him asking the children to go and find their mother.

"Franz Bielke. The ambassador? Nils' uncle? He's been murdered."

There was a long silence. Then, "Good God. Bielke? Murdered, you say?"

"Yes. I just found him. In the garden. No one knows yet. Except the murderer I suppose. But it's complicated. There are some things I should tell you before the police arrive and they start asking questions."

"Um, what sort of things, Maggie?" William was cautious. He had noticed the attention Bielke had been paying to Maggie and his father's reaction to it.

"Nothing I'd want to say over the phone. But I promise I had nothing to do with Bielke's death. And I'm sure your father didn't either."

William sighed.

"All right. I'll leave right away."

"I'm going to call Inspector Willis. And then tell your father."

"He doesn't know?"

"Not yet. No."

The call ended.

Maggie hesitated. She took a deep breath, then dialled another number she knew by heart. After a few rings, it was answered.

"Inspector Willis? It's Maggie. Eliot. Er. Raynham."

There was a pause. The inspector answered cautiously, "Hello, Maggie."

"Inspector, I wish I were calling you simply to wish you a merry Christmas. Which I do. Except I'm not."

After Willis had puzzled out what she had said, he asked, "Then why are you calling, Maggie? Don't tell me you've found another dead body?"

Maggie sighed. The man thought he was making a joke.

"Yes. I'm afraid that's exactly why I'm calling."

Willis was speechless.

"And he's not only dead. He's been murdered. Quite brutally. At Beaumatin. In the gardens. And I know who it is."

"So who is he? Your victim."

"A Swede. Named Franz Bielke. A truly vile man. He's the uncle of Nils von Fersen, who married Thomas' daughter Constance yesterday. You've met Constance. He, Bielke that is, was here for the wedding. With the rest of Nils' family."

"All right, Maggie." She could tell Willis was trying to speak calmly.

"The pathologist and the SOCOs will arrive soon. Well, as soon as they can get out to your place. And Sergeant Patrick and I and some police constables will also come. But meanwhile, can you keep everyone inside? Out of the gardens? And not say anything until we get there?"

"I can try. I should probably tell Thomas, though."

"Yes. I remember. His lordship likes to be kept informed."

"Let me go and tell him, then."

The call ended.

Maggie reluctantly left Bielke's body and went back to the house. She found Thomas pacing in the hall.

"Where have you been? Lunch is ready. Everyone's waiting."

"Then they'll just have to wait."

Maggie pulled Thomas into her study. He looked more closely. There was a dark reddish smear on her cheek. And more on the jacket. On a pocket. On a sleeve. On the bottom hem. On her trousers. The knees. And the cuffs. And the toes of her boots.

"Maggie, what is that? Is it blood?"

Maggie nodded.

"It's Bielke's. He's dead."

"Dead? How? Did you kill him? Was it an accident? Were you shooting…"

"No. I didn't kill him. Someone else did. He's been murdered."

"What?"

"I found him. In the far garden. Near the early snowdrops. He'd been…"

Maggie drew a finger across her throat, then mimicked thrusting her fingers up under her rib cage.

"With a trowel."

Thomas looked like he was thinking several things at once and none were pleasant.

"I called William. I thought it would be good if he were here. And I called Inspector Willis."

"Willis." Thomas did not like the Inspector.

"He said to keep everyone inside. In the same place, if possible. And not to tell them what's happened."

"Well everyone is in the dining room. Waiting for you," he added.

"I can't go in like this," Maggie said reasonably.

Thomas frowned at Maggie's blood-stained clothes.

"I guess you can't. Let me go make your excuses. Tell them to start. And I want to go see…"

"I don't think you should, Thomas."

"Afraid I'll defile your dead lover's body?" he snapped.

Maggie recoiled.

"Thomas! He wasn't…"

But he had gone.

Derek walked in.

"Maggie! Merry Christmas. Or the day before the day before Christmas. Damien and I are de-decorating the ballroom. Maggie? What's that on you?"

"It's blood, Derek. I found another body."

"Blood? Euuwww. Damien, Maggie's found another body," Derek called out into the hall.

"Shh. No one's supposed to know."

"Not even the police?"

"The police know. They're the ones who said not to tell anyone."

"Oops. Sorry."

Damien strolled in.

"Hi, Maggie. What's this about a body?"

"It's one of the Swedes. That vile Franz Bielke."

Damien thought. "Tall? Blond? Haughty? Has a scar? Sort of Scandi-does-Thomas?"

"That's the one. I found his body. He's been murdered. His throat was slashed open. And…"

Maggie suddenly felt like she needed to sit down.

"Maggie? Are you all right? Can I get you some tea?" Derek wrung his hands.

"Some brandy?" asked the more practical Damien.

"No. Thank you. I'll be all right. It was just very… gruesome."

"Well I would think so," agreed Derek.

"And very convenient. For me. So perhaps it was convenient for someone else as well. But whom?" Maggie thought.

But was it convenient? Because now who would tell Thomas that Bielke hadn't been in her room. Except now, of course, he had been. And would Thomas ever believe her?

Chapter 16

The pathologist, the SOCOs and Detective Inspector Willis arrived simultaneously. Maggie saw them pull up in front of the house from her study windows and was glad the windows of the dining room, where the von Fersens were finishing lunch, looked out to the other side of the house.

Thomas had returned and, except for a curt "I'll be in the dining room," had said nothing more to her.

Maggie went out to greet the police. Willis got out of dark Ford Mondeo, driven by his sergeant, Jack Patrick, and grimaced when he saw Maggie and her bloody clothes. Four other police constables emerged from two police cars.

"If you'd show us where the body is. And then you'll need to go with an officer and hand over what you're wearing."

Willis was in his forties but looked older. Maggie's height, he had grizzled grey-brown hair, hooded grey eyes and a sturdy build. A well-worn Burberry trench coat covered a business-like grey suit.

Maggie nodded and escorted everyone to the far garden where Bielke was lying. The rain had already washed much of the blood away.

Willis scowled.

"Is this how he was when you found him?"

Maggie nodded. "Except there's less blood. The rain…"

"Owens, would you go with Lady Raynham so she can give you her clothes?" Willis asked a WPC.

"Then I'll go talk to… what's their name again?"

"The von Fersens. There are ten of them, plus Constance and Nils. Oh. Sorry. I guess there are now nine. Thomas is with them as well. If you'd come to my study first, I can give you a list. I'll wait."

Willis nodded. "I won't be long."

PC Owens went back to the house with Maggie. She stopped in the kitchen where Mrs Cook had already noticed the arrival of the police. The housekeeper stared at Maggie.

"Lady Raynham. Are you all right? What's happened?"

"Mrs Cook. I'm afraid there's been an… an accident. Ambassador Bielke. Inspector Willis… You remember Inspector Willis?"

Mrs Cook nodded grimly.

"He asked that nothing be said until he has had a chance to talk to the von Fersens personally. Lord Raynham is with them. When they have finished with lunch, perhaps they could have coffee and tea in the drawing room. Inspector Willis can meet with them there. And I'll join them. Once I've changed."

Maggie led PC Owens up a back stairway to her room. She didn't particularly care what the woman thought of the exotic furnishings. She quickly gave everything that she was wearing, including her boots, to the officer, then washed her face and pulled on a clean pair of jeans, a navy cashmere turtleneck sweater and loafers.

PS Owens put Maggie's clothes and boots in a large plastic bag and left. Maggie went down to her study to wait for Willis.

Five minutes later, Willis appeared. He looked grumpy.

Maggie handed him the list Gweneth had given her.

"Nils' family. At least the ones who are here. Minus Ambassador Bielke. Oh, and Agneta Ekeblad is pregnant."

"This is everyone?"

"Our staff you know. There have been no changes. Except Mrs Griggs and Mrs Bateson, who live in the village, have been coming in to help Mrs Cook. I don't know if they've been in today or not. You'll need to ask Mrs Cook.

"Derek Fiske and Damien Hawking are garden designers and have a garden centre in Burford. They're in the ballroom taking down the decorations from the dance that was held here last night. In fact, I believe you may have met them previously as well.

"Oh. And then there's Lionel Trueblood-Fitch. He's a reporter from *Country Style* magazine and is here covering the wedding. And his photographer. Knowles. Hmm. That's strange."

"What's strange?"

"Just that I've seen neither of them today. Usually, well, Trueblood-Fitch seems to have developed a crush on Derek and tends to hang around wherever he is, much to Damien's annoyance."

Willis' shoulders slumped. He straightened and asked, "The drawing room, you said?"

Maggie nodded.

Willis went out into the hall. The police constables were waiting, as well as Sergeant Patrick.

"Patrick, come with me. The rest of you, wait here. Stay alert."

Willis entered the drawing room. Twelve pairs of eyes met his. Maggie slipped in behind the detectives and tried to blend into a wall, out of sight of the Swedes.

"I'm Detective Inspector Willis of the Gloucestershire CID and this is Detective Sergeant Patrick. I appreciate that you are probably wondering what is going on."

He paused.

"I'm afraid I must inform you that Franz Bielke was murdered late this morning."

There was complete silence. Maggie glanced at Thomas, who was standing across the room. He deliberately looked away from her.

Anna Sofia was the first to react.

"Ah. I understand. This is one of these English country house games. Someone pretends to be killed and then we must find out who is guilty. This is one of your entertainments, Constance. Yes?"

Constance looked confused.

Ulrika von Fersen spoke. "No, I do not believe it is a game, Anna Sofia. Is it, Inspector Willis?"

"I'm afraid not, er, Mrs von Fersen." He took a chance on the name.

"Not a game," Anna Sofia was processing this.

"You mean Franz is dead? My Franz is dead? Oh no. No. It is not possible!"

The woman began to sob hysterically.

Maggie approached the Inspector.

"Perhaps Mrs von Fersen…"

Willis nodded at Patrick, who called in PC Owens.

Still sobbing, Anna Sofia was led from the room.

Maggie noticed Constance was also looking like she was going to lose it.

"Inspector Willis, would it be all right if I waited in my study?"

He nodded and Maggie left. As she closed the door, she heard him explaining that he would need to talk to each of them individually, that it was just a matter of routine, that PCs Richards and Holmes would stay with them and that if there was anything anyone needed, they should just ask one of the police constables.

Maggie was still in the hall when Willis came out.

"Er, Maggie?"

"Inspector?"

"I'll need a place to hold interviews."

"The library? I believe you've used it before," she smiled.

Willis looked morose. He had indeed used the library before and he remembered the interviews.

"And as you're the one who found the body…" the "again" was unspoken, "I'd like to speak with you first."

"Of course. But I have called William Conyers, whom you also know, and I need to confer with him before we talk," said Maggie, to Willis' surprise.

"So please get settled. If there is anything you need, Sergeant Patrick can ask Mrs Cook. And I promise I will be with you shortly."

Maggie went into her study and left Willis looking after her and frowning.

Chapter 17

Maggie found William waiting in her study. He did not look happy.

"Well? Is it true? Ambassador Bielke was murdered? In the garden?"

"Yes. And I found him. Someone had taken a trowel and, er, slashed his throat with it and then driven it into his chest."

William looked even more unhappy.

"William, everything I tell you is confidential, isn't it?"

"Yes," William answered warily.

"All right. Then first you should know that I did not kill Bielke. And I'm sure your father didn't either. However, there are issues…"

"Issues?"

Maggie sighed.

"Yes. Issues. I guess the biggest is… Bielke was trying to blackmail me."

"What?"

Maggie explained about Bielke's pursuit of her. And Thomas' growing anger. Then the kiss in the ballroom and Thomas' punching Bielke.

"But isn't there some rule about a wife not being forced to give evidence against her husband?"

"Yes."

"Then it's all right if I don't mention that part? About Thomas punching Bielke? To the police?"

William was looking dumbfounded, but managed, "No, you don't have to."

"Good."

She continued with Thomas' assuming she had wanted Bielke to kiss her and his saying they were finished.

"It's really difficult. Having all these people here. I don't feel like I have the chance to talk him down or clear the air with a knock-down, drag-out fight."

William nodded. He knew his father's tendency to jump to conclusions. Especially where Maggie was concerned.

Maggie finished with the scene outside her bedroom door and Bielke's visit of that morning and the blackmail.

"I must be the first person ever to be blackmailed for not having an affair," Maggie mused.

"Anyway, I told Bielke to go to hell. But from what he said. I was not his only victim. Or intended victim. So…."

"So…"

"So maybe the murderer is someone else Bielke was trying to blackmail. But the problem is, besides the murder, I mean, is that Inspector Willis… Well, you remember Inspector Willis."

William nodded. He remembered Inspector Willis. And his memories were not pleasant.

"He and your father. Well, I don't think they like each other. At all. And I'm afraid…"

"You're afraid that, because Willis dislikes my father, he'll focus on him as a suspect?"

"Yes. That's it exactly. And that it will distract him from finding the real murderer."

William nodded. And reflected that, whether or not Willis disliked his father, the policeman would have perfectly good, objective reasons for targeting him as a suspect.

"So here's what I intend to do."

Maggie explained her plan. Then she paused.

"What is it, Maggie?"

"Well, it's strange, is all. Who kills someone with a garden trowel?"

William had no answer to that.

SUSAN ALEXANDER

Chapter 18

Maggie was sitting in the library with William, Willis and Patrick.

"Very déja vu," she remarked.

Willis grimaced.

"Very well, Mag..., Lady Rayn..."

"Maggie is fine, Inspector," she interrupted and smiled at the detective.

"Could you please tell me how you came to find Mr Bielke's body?"

"All right. Although formally I think it's more proper to refer to him as Ambassador Bielke," Maggie pointed out.

That earned her a "whatever" look from Willis.

"I wanted to get some fresh air and went out to take a walk in the gardens. I found Ambassador Bielke lying near the early-blooming snowdrops, in one of the areas farthest from the house. He was lying on his back. He had had his throat... I'd say slashed but it was much messier. And a garden trowel was sticking... it looked like it had been thrust up under his ribs into his chest. There was blood everywhere. Well, I assume you saw it. Him."

"But it was raining, wasn't it? You went for a walk in the rain? You didn't mind getting wet?"

"I know. But this is England. It's always raining. And I'm not the Wicked Witch of the West from *The Wizard of Oz*. I don't melt when I get a little water on me."

She smiled at the inspector, but he did not smile back.

"So what did you do?"

"I felt his neck to see if there were a pulse."

"But it must have been fairly obvious he was dead."

"Yes. But I wanted to make sure."

"You wanted to make sure he was dead?"

"Yes."

William gave Maggie a look when she said that. She shrugged.

"And is that how you came to have Mr Bielke's blood all over you?"

"All over?"

"Your face, your jacket, your pants, your boots. Even your mobile. Wouldn't you say that was all over?"

"I'd say that I had blood on my face, my jacket, my pants, my boots and my mobile," said Maggie the exacting academic.

"Very well. Then what did you do?"

"I called you. I called Mr Conyers. Then I went to find Thomas and tell him. Because you had asked me…"

"Let's take things one at a time, er, Maggie," Willis interrupted.

"You called me. And when you called me, you called Bielke 'that vile man.' Why did you call him that?"

Maggie relaxed back in her chair and crossed her long legs. Time to channel Sharon Stone. She had seen *Basic Instinct* at an impressionable age—well, she had been in her thirties—and for her Stone's performance during her police interview was synonymous with "grace under pressure."

"Because he was blackmailing me," she said simply.

Willis dropped the pen he was using to take notes in surprise and Patrick gaped.

William, who had known what was coming, looked pained.

"Blackmailing you?" Willis finally managed.

"Yes."

"Over what?"

"He wanted me to give him £20,000 to tell Thomas that we were not having an affair."

Willis almost dropped his pen again.

"He wanted money so he wouldn't tell Lord Raynham that you were having an affair?"

"No. No. Because we weren't. Having an affair. But there had been one or two… incidents. Which might have led Thomas to believe… So Bielke wanted me to pay him so he would tell Thomas the truth. That there was no affair.

"Although he seemed to be flexible on payment terms. And price. He thought as I was a poorly-paid professor I might find it hard to get £20,000. He said he would accept a payment plan. Like when you buy a car. Or that I could give him some of the Raynham diamonds and he could have a friend who is a jeweller replace them with fakes stones.

"Finally he proposed that I give him £10,000 and he would take the rest in… well, that I would… And then in fact we would have been… Not that that was ever going to happen. Anyway, as I said, he was a vile man. And he said blackmailing people was how he supplemented his pension. So I assume I was not his only victim. Or intended victim."

Willis looked gobsmacked. He tried to collect himself.

"When did this happen? This demand for money?"

"This morning."

"Where were you?"

"I had just finished taking a shower. I came out of my bathroom and found him in my bedroom. I was tired and had forgotten to lock the door. Although you'd think it would be a reasonable assumption that someone wouldn't enter unless… Anyway, he proceeded to, I guess you could say to make me an offer he thought I couldn't refuse."

"And did you?"

"Did I?"

"Accept his offer."

Maggie looked surprised.

"No. Of course not. I told him to get out and go to hell."

Willis stared at Maggie. She looked back at him calmly. But she had had exactly the same look on previous occasions when he had subsequently found out she had been lying through her teeth.

"And what did he say? Usually blackmailers make threats."

"He said not only would he not tell Thomas we were not having an affair… Oh dear. Sorry about the dodgy grammar. That he would carry on so that Thomas would be sure to believe that we were. Having an affair. Bielke said he'd have broken up my marriage by New Year's. Although in fact I think he was overestimating. I would only have given it until Christmas," she added thoughtfully.

"That's the day after tomorrow," Willis pointed out.

"Yes. It is."

"So his death was convenient for you."

"Yes. It was. Very."

Willis looked hard at Maggie. Did she realise what she was saying?

He referred to his notes.

"You mentioned there had been incidents. What were they?"

"Well first, I'm not sure it could be called an incident, but ever since he arrived, Bielke had been flirting. Been too familiar. Paid too much attention. Stood too close. Been inappropriately physical. It was quite noticeable."

"Why didn't you tell him then to, er, 'go to hell?'"

"Because he was a guest in our house. His sister is the mother of Constance's fiancé, er, husband. And Anna

Sofia seems to be very attached to her brother. Perhaps even overly attached. Given how evil he was. Anyhow, I didn't want to cause a scene and, er, create tension or do anything to affect the wedding."

"And did Lord Raynham notice? What was his reaction?"

"He was unhappy about it."

It was Willis' opinion that Maggie's husband was pathologically jealous, but he kept that to himself and thought, "Unhappy my ass."

"And the other incidents?"

"I was in the ballroom. The day before the wedding. Bielke came in and… kissed me."

"Kissed you?"

"Yes. And I had made it quite clear I did not want to be kissed. By him."

"Bielke, er, forced himself on you."

"Yes."

"And what happened next?"

"Thomas came in."

Maggie glanced at William. He nodded. A wife was not obliged to give evidence her husband if she chose not to.

"Thomas saw Bielke kissing me and he thought it was consensual. He, er, we went into his study and Thomas said… he said that I had to, er, keep up appearances until after the wedding but then it was over. We were finished."

Willis failed to hide his shock. He quickly looked down at his notes.

"You didn't tell him what actually happened?"

"I tried. But he didn't believe me. Given Bielke's previous pattern of behaviour."

Willis remembered that this was not the first time Raynham had not listened to his wife and jumped to a wrong conclusion.

"And was there anything else?" he continued.

"Yes. Yesterday afternoon. After the wedding. I was taking a shower. Bielke came to my room. He tried to get in but the door was locked. Fortunately. However, Thomas saw him and Bielke let him think he had just been leaving. After a lovers' assignation. That's what he wanted me to pay him for. To tell Thomas he had not in fact been in my room.

"Although of course, now that I think about it, I have only Bielke's word that that's what happened. He could have been making it up. I was in the shower, as I said, and cannot be sure just what may have gone on," Maggie added thoughtfully.

Willis' face became expressionless.

"Tell me, Lady Raynham. Where were you when Bielke was killed'?"

Maggie noticed Willis had switched from 'Maggie' to 'Lady Raynham.' She smiled to herself.

"I don't know, Inspector Willis. When was he killed?"

"Between ten o'clock and just after noon, then."

"Or between the time he left my room and the time I called you?"

"Yes."

"So am I the famous, or infamous, last person to have seen the victim alive as well as the person who found the body? Oh my."

"If you would please answer the question."

"After Bielke left I went down to get some coffee from Mrs Cook. At some point the von Fersens returned. They had gone to visit Tetbury but apparently felt it was too wet to continue with their little tour. Although it was not too wet to have done some shopping. Anyway, I had a bit of cabin fever, so I decided to go out. That's when I found Bielke. I am not sure about exact times."

"So you have no alibi."

"It seems not."

"Did you see Lord Raynham at all during this period?"

Maggie thought.

"Bielke told me Thomas had gone out with Ned. I see no reason he would not have been truthful about that. I did not see Thomas myself until I came in from having found Bielke. He was in the hall. He wasn't wearing riding clothes, so he must have changed. He was looking for me. Evidentially my absence was holding up lunch."

"You did not see him in the garden while you were there?"

"No. I did not."

Maggie looked right at Willis and he believed she was telling the truth. At least about this.

"Do you love your husband, Lady Raynham?"

"Yes. I do," Maggie said without hesitation.

"And Bielke was trying to destroy your marriage."

"Yes. He was."

"You could even say he was succeeding."

"Yes. He was succeeding."

Willis again wondered if Maggie realised what she was saying.

"You would have been ruined."

Now Maggie laughed.

"I am still a professor at Oxford, Inspector Willis. If adultery and divorce were grounds for dismissal, there would hardly be any faculty left at all."

Willis persisted.

"But Bielke had convinced your husband, the man you say you love, that you were having an affair. And Lord Raynham had told you that the two of you were finished. That your marriage was over."

"Yes. That is correct."

"Did you murder Franz Bielke, Lady Raynham?"

Maggie looked at William, who said what he had agreed to say.

Susan Alexander

"Lady Raynham is not going to answer that question, Inspector."

Chapter 19

Back in her study, Maggie turned to William.

"Well, that went well."

"You think so? Because you convinced Willis that you may be the one who murdered Bielke?"

Maggie sighed.

"At least he's not completely convinced that your father murdered Bielke. And since he didn't, we don't want Willis believing that he did. Especially since he seems not to like your father very much. I thought we agreed about this."

William still looked unhappy.

"I had better go talk to my father."

"Yes. I am sure you should be there when the inspector questions him. But please, don't say anything about what I've told you."

"I shouldn't tell him about the blackmail?"

"No. But only because I doubt that he'd believe you. He seems unwilling to listen to anything I have to say at the moment. I don't think your telling him would make a difference and probably only make him angry with you as well."

William had to agree that Maggie was undoubtedly right about his father.

"Very well. But what if Inspector Willis tells him?"

Maggie shrugged. "There's nothing I can do about that. Although somehow I don't think he will. At least about the blackmail."

William left.

Maggie went into the hall. She heard noises from the ballroom and went to investigate.

Derek was up on a ladder taking down the clouds of tulle and handing them to Damien, who was folding them carefully. The forest of white, glittery branches that had lined the walls were already gathered and tied in bundles.

"Hi, guys."

"Hi, Maggie."

"Keep calm and carry on, that's us."

"Have you spoken with Inspector Willis?"

"No. But we did speak with his sergeant. Each of us. Individually. Since we're each other's alibi. I guess he wanted to see if our stories matched," explained Damien.

"And that Sergeant Patrick's a real cutie," added Derek.

"Really, Derek!"

"Well he is, Day," insisted Derek.

"Anyway, I gather we were in here working during the critical period," Damien continued.

"Hear no evil, see no evil, speak no evil," agreed Derek.

"Especially since that Trueblood-Fitch wasn't here hanging around Derek for once," added Damien.

"Really?" Maggie wondered if this were significant.

"If he calls me 'my dear boy' one more time…" said Derek.

"Anyway, I was wondering… Well, could you take a break for a few minutes? I wanted to talk to you. I could use your help."

"Anything for Maggie. Eliot. Er, Raynham." Derek mimicked Maggie.

Damien nodded.

"Oh dear, I guess I do say that," she said ruefully.

Derek climbed down the ladder.

"Well, that's thirsty work. Tea for you, Day? And coffee for Maggie, of course."

"Um. Would you mind asking Mrs Cook? Have her bring it to my study? I'm trying to avoid the von Fersens. As they seem to think either Thomas or I is responsible. For Bielke's death."

"No!" Derek was outraged.

"But why?" wondered Damien.

"I'll tell you everything as soon as we have some tea. And coffee."

A stoic Mrs Cook brought in a tray with tea and coffee to Maggie's study. To show her support she had added a plate of her miniature mince pies.

"Thank you, Mrs Cook," Maggie said.

Derek was already trying one of the pies.

"Oh my. These are good."

Mrs Cook smiled unconvincingly, then left.

"So tell us," said Derek.

"Well. The short version is that I guess you could say Bielke has been doing the same thing with me as Trueblood-Fitch has been doing with you, Derek. Being inappropriate. In front of Thomas. Only, unlike you, Damien, Thomas thought I was encouraging… that I wanted Bielke to… behave the way he was behaving. And then the day before the wedding, I was in the ballroom and Bielke kissed me. Even though he knew I didn't want him to. And Thomas came in and saw him. Us. He punched Bielke. And he wouldn't listen to me when I tried to explain.

"And then Thomas thought he saw Bielke coming out of my bedroom. Except he wasn't, of course. But Bielke convinced him that he was. And then Bielke wanted me to give him money to tell Thomas what was really going on. Which was nothing. At least on my side."

"He was blackmailing you?" Damien was outraged.

Maggie nodded.

What a villain," said Derek.

"What can we do?" asked Damien.

"Well. What I'm afraid of is that Inspector Willis will think Thomas killed Bielke. I'm sure he didn't, but I'm also sure Willis will think he did. And I can't talk to the von Fersens. Because like I said, they also seem to think Thomas killed that awful man. Or that I did. And they certainly believe I'm to blame for what happened. So what I was hoping was that maybe you could play detectives. See what you can find out."

Damien hesitated.

"Oh come on, Day. Maggie needs us. And it will be fun. Well, fun except that it's serious, of course."

"Well…" Damien was reluctant.

"You'll be here anyway. And the von Fersens can't leave because of the murder. Well you know how that goes." Maggie was encouraging.

"Yes we do," said Derek.

"Who do you think did it?"

"It's like that awful man. Mitch. Bielke would have been my first choice of evil doer. Except obviously he didn't murder himself. My working hypothesis is that he was trying to blackmail someone else. And that was the person who killed him."

"And you're sure it wasn't Thomas?" Damien ventured.

"No. It was absolutely not Thomas," said Maggie firmly.

"All right. If you say so," said Derek, with less conviction than Maggie would have liked.

"My, these mince pies are good, though," he said as he helped himself to another.

Susan Alexander

Chapter 20

Willis was questioning Lionel Trueblood-Fitch. Patrick had told him the man was a society reporter for some posh magazine. Certainly not one he had ever read. And even with his limited fashion sense, Willis was sure the man's jacket of lime green, navy and grey tweed was in bad taste. He would have to ask Patrick, who knew about these things.

"So, Mr Trueblood-Fitch. Can you tell me where you were this morning?"

"I slept in. The festivities yesterday were just too exhausting. Then I got up and started to pack. I have to leave this afternoon. I have a new assignment that starts on Boxing Day. The Earl and Countess of…"

Willis cut him off.

"I'm afraid no one can leave Beaumatin at present, Mr Trueblood-Fitch. You'll need to make other arrangements."

"Oh dear. The Earl and Countess…"

"So you were in your room. You didn't go with the others to, er, Tetbury I believe it was?"

"No. I'm no tourist. And those people. Those Swedes. So dreary. Do you think it's the weather? All those months with no sun? Or maybe it's that awful diet. Herring? In curry sauce? Please."

"So you never left your room?"

"Only to get some tea."

"Can anyone confirm that?"

"That wonderful housekeeper Raynham has gave me the tea."

"And can anyone confirm that you were in your room?"

"Only my suitcase. All packed. Ready to go."

"Well, you'll need to unpack. Until we've resolved some… issues."

Willis consulted his notes.

"So Mr Trueblood-Fitch. You're a journalist. You were observing all these people. What did you think of Mr Bielke?"

"Ambassador Bielke, you mean? Not a very nice man. At least to a lowly rapporteur who was only trying to do his job. Arrogant. Unpleasant. Snobbish."

"Not the friendly type."

"Not to me. Of course, it was different with Lady Raynham."

"Yes?"

"He seemed quite, um, interested in her."

"Interested?"

"The way a man like that would be interested in someone else's wife. Sexually interested."

"In love?"

Trueblood-Fitch laughed. "Oh please. The only person someone like Bielke loves is himself. But he liked the hunt. The pursuit. He had a big ego. And doing it in front of Lord Raynham. It made it even more appealing.

"Plus, in my experience, put two alpha males in the same space and you can expect to have some sort of pissing contest. Whether it's about who'll win the Premiership or which year of Chateau Margaux is better. In this case it happened to be Lady Raynham. The fact that she so obviously loves Raynham just made it a bigger challenge for Bielke."

"And was he succeeding? In his pursuit? To your knowledge?"

"I don't know if he was succeeding with Lady Raynham. But with his lordship? Raynham was completely enraged. Knowles has some pictures. I can have him show you if you like."

"Please."

"And then there was that incident yesterday afternoon…"

"Yes? What incident?"

"It was after the wedding. And the wedding lunch. People were either resting or getting ready for the ball. You know about the ball? The dance that was held here? I was on my way downstairs. And just happened to be passing Lady Raynham's room. Bielke was outside her door. He knocked. He didn't get a response. He tried the knob. The door seemed to be locked.

"Bielke was about to turn away when Lord Raynham came around the corner. He saw Bielke at Lady Raynham's door. When Bielke saw Raynham, he put his hand on the door knob as though he had just closed it. As though he had just come out of Lady Raynham's bedroom.

"Raynham went white. I thought he would go for Bielke for sure. He looked murderous. Oh dear. I guess it's indiscrete of me to say that. Under the circumstances.

"And Bielke just smiled at Raynham. It was pure evil. Nothing was said. Bielke just turned and walked away. Nearly knocked me over," said Trueblood-Fitch indignantly.

"And Raynham?"

"He went back the way he'd come, I think. I'm not certain. It was all rather fraught."

Willis was doodling on his notepad.

Finally he said, "Those pictures. May I send Sergeant Patrick with you to get them?"

"Of course. Anything I can do to help the police."

Chapter 21

Four men were sitting in the library. Willis, Patrick, Thomas and William.

"So Lord Raynham. There's been a murder at this place of yours. Again."

Thomas said nothing. The antipathy between the two men was palpable. It did not surprise Sergeant Patrick, who thought his lordship was a stuck-up prig and assumed his superior shared his feelings, but it concerned William. Why would his father and the inspector hate each other? It seemed that Maggie was right to be worried.

"Can you give me an account of your whereabouts this morning?"

"I rode out with my estate foreman, Ned Thatcher, at nine o'clock. I returned around eleven. I changed, went to my study, began to do some accounting. Our houseguests returned from their tour early. Apparently they thought it was too wet to be out. They went… I suppose to their rooms. They were informed that a lunch would be served. According to the original plan they were to eat at some hotel in Tetbury, I believe. I went back to my study. At 12:30 I went to the dining room.

"Ambassador Bielke and Lady Raynham…" Thomas paused at the linkage of the two names. "They had not appeared. People were waiting. I went to look for Lady Raynham. I was in the hall when she came and told me about Bielke's murder."

"Very well. When you were working in your study, can anyone confirm this?"

Thomas thought. "No. I was undisturbed."

"And did you have any occasion to go into your gardens this morning?"

"No. When I rode out, it was to the fields. Mr Thatcher can confirm that."

"So you did not go into the gardens at all today?"

"Only after Lady Raynham told me that Ambassador Bielke had been murdered."

"So you went to…."

"It seemed extraordinary to me, what Lady Raynham said. I went to see for myself."

"And did you see?"

"Yes. I saw. Er, that Ambassador Bielke had been murdered."

"And did you see Mr Bielke at any other time today? Except after he was dead?"

"No. I did not."

"You're certain?"

"Yes. Quite certain."

Willis pretended to review his notes while he considered his strategy. Finally he said, "What did you think of Mr Bielke?"

"What did I think?"

"Yes. What kind of man was he? How did he strike you?"

Thomas frowned.

"I had only met him a few days ago. He had had a distinguished career as a diplomat. He was my son-in-law's uncle."

"He knew his fish knife from his butter knife, is what you're saying? He fit in. With your sort," Willis said.

Willis had not asked a question. Thomas said nothing.

Willis continued "And is it also okay with 'your sort,' for a man to try to seduce his host's wife?"

Thomas stiffened.

"I'd appreciate an answer, Lord Raynham," Willis persisted.

"No. No, it is not," Thomas finally managed.

"But he did, nonetheless. From nearly the moment he arrived, if my understanding is correct. From what people have said. How did you feel about this? What was your reaction?"

Thomas was silent.

"I asked a question, Lord Raynham."

"You asked two," interjected William.

"Then answer both please."

"I found his behaviour… objectionable."

"I'm sure you did. So what did you do about it? You couldn't challenge him to a duel, as I'm sure some of those ancestors you've got hanging up on the walls here would have done. How did you defend your wife's, er, honour?"

Thomas flushed.

"He was a guest in my house. There was the wedding. I did not want to create a scene…"

"So you did nothing?"

Thomas was silent.

"Perhaps you did nothing because Lady Raynham did not find Bielke so… objectionable."

Thomas clenched and unclenched his fists.

"Did you speak to Lady Raynham about this?"

Thomas was about to answer but William put his hand on his father's arm.

"Lord Raynham is not going to answer that question, Inspector."

"What did she tell you about Bielke and his attentions? That they were unwanted? Or perhaps that they were not unwanted?"

"Lord Raynham is not going to answer that question, Inspector."

"Very well. Tell me this, then. Yesterday afternoon, you saw Bielke. In the hall outside your wife's bedroom. He was apparently just leaving. The wedding was safely over. Do you really expect me to believe you did nothing?"

"Lord Raynham is not going to…"

"Answer that question. Right."

Wolcum Yole

Willis stood.

"We are conducting a thorough search of your… place. The murder was a messy business. The killer could not have avoided getting bloody."

Willis frowned as he said that and thought of Maggie.

"So we would like all your guests to stay downstairs, in the dining room and drawing room, until we have finished. And you and Lady Raynham can have access to your studies. I believe the SOCOs have already finished there. But please don't leave the house. I will doubtless have some further questions. Even if you are not inclined to provide any answers."

Chapter 22

After Thomas and William left, Willis sat down and looked at his sergeant.

"Let's take a moment to think about things before we go any further," he proposed.

"So far, we have two people with obvious motives for killing Bielke. The Raynhams. Lord Raynham because he's a jealous sod and Bielke's seduced his wife. Or he thinks he has seduced her. And Lady Raynham, who was being victimised by Bielke. If we believe her."

"If we believe her, sir?"

"She's an accomplished liar, is Lady Raynham. Remember that case at the convent? She'd look me straight in the eye and swear she'd told me everything there was to know, when she was holding the most important bits back."

"That's obstructing an investigation, sir. You didn't charge her?"

"No. She was covered by that Scotland Yard DCI. Dexter."

"So you think she's lying now?"

"Or not telling the whole story."

Willis thought.

"We need to know if Bielke actually did seduce her. If he did, there may still be some forensic evidence. Tell the SOCOs to go over her and Bielke's rooms with a fine toothed comb for pubic hair, traces of fluids, fingerprints, everything.

"And maybe she'd consent to having a rape kit run. Ask her. Bielke could have forced her."

Patrick looked alarmed.

Me, sir? Couldn't you? It seems she'd be more likely to…"

"Oh. Right. You're probably right. I'll do it. Even if she refuses, her reaction might tell us something."

Willis flipped through his notes.

"Although there's one problem with Lady Raynham as our murderess. That trowel. In my experience, she'd be much more likely to have shot Bielke. And there's no shortage of guns in the house. That trowel is more a man's instrument. That took strength. And to drive it into his chest like that. After his throat had been cut. That was pure viciousness. I'm not sure I can see her ladyship doing that."

"Unless she was fighting him off."

"Perhaps. Although that would be a strange place for Bielke to attack her. In the rain. The ground all mucky."

"Maybe he was just seizing an opportunity?"

"Maybe. Although then why didn't she say it was self-defence? Anyway, you've reminded me. There'll be footprints. Bielke's. The Raynhams'. And perhaps a fourth set. If the rain hasn't messed them up. Let's see if we can figure out who turned up in what order. If we find one of Lady Raynham's prints superimposed on one of Raynham's, that would knock his story that he hadn't been in the gardens earlier all to bits."

Patrick made a note.

"And then, if Bielke was a blackmailer, maybe he was blackmailing someone else. Let's see if there's anyone here who's likely."

Willis rubbed his hand over his eyes.

"And then there's Raynham. He's the obvious suspect. Jealous husband thinks wife's having an affair whether she is or not. He kills the lover. And like I said, he is a jealous sod. And has no real alibi. And they're his gardens. That trowel…"

Willis thought.

"See if you can find out if he's been violent before. Ask around. Try Draycott. Stephen Draycott. You know who he is. And Mag, er, Lady Raynham's friend Anne Brooks. Lives in Broadway. Maybe her ladyship confided in her. Maybe she even talked about Bielke. Women tell each other these things, don't they?

"And there's Stanley Einhorn. Although he might be hard to contact. Try anyway. And she has that friend at Oxford who's a professor. Kazi, or something like that. See what there is to find out."

"Although it seems Lady Raynham's got just as good a motive, sir. And no alibi either."

"Yes. She pretty much handed herself to us on a platter. As a suspect. Why would she do that? She's smart. A lot smarter than you or me. She'd thought through what she was going to say. And what she wasn't. She'd prepped that lawyer, too. Conyers. Raynham's son. Heir. He supported her.

"And that story about Bielke blackmailing her. We've only got her word. There's no proof at all. It's not like he sent her a letter with a compromising picture. Although, then again, why would she make something like that up?"

"To give herself a motive?"

Willis sat up. "You may be on to something there. But why?"

"Oh that one's easy, sir. To protect her husband. She thinks he did it."

Chapter 23

Maggie and William were conferring about what to do about the von Fersens when Sergeant Patrick knocked on her study door.

"Inspector Willis would like to see you in your bedroom, Lady Raynham. If you please."

"Would you come too, please, William?" Maggie asked.

They went upstairs.

Maggie was not worried about a police search. She had taken the jacket and tie Thomas had left in her room down to Mrs Cook when she had gone to get coffee earlier. Any other traces of Thomas would be normal.

It was the first time William had been in Maggie's bedroom since she had re-decorated it. He remembered it from when it had been his mother's, done in pink and blue chintz, patterned in butterflies and flowers.

William stopped dead on the threshold.

"Welcome to the seraglio," Maggie murmured.

"You wished to see me, Inspector?" Maggie asked.

Willis was also looking bemused. At the large room containing only the outrageous pagoda-roofed bed with its gilded dragons rampant, a massive, ornate mirror leaning against one wall and a couple of chairs.

Willis pulled himself together.

"Yes. Er, Lady Raynham, is this your dress?"

Maggie had removed Thomas' clothes but had overlooked her ball gown, which was still lying on the floor.

"Yes. I wore it to the dance that was held here last night."

Willis lifted part of the dress with gloved hands to reveal rips and tears.

"And was it like this when you wore it? Is this a new fashion trend I've missed? The posh punk look?"

William saw the state of the dress and tried to hide his shock. What had happened?

"No, it is not. It was not."

"So who did this? How did it happen?"

Maggie nudged the barrister.

"Lady Raynham is not going to answer that question, Inspector."

Willis' face hardened.

"Very well. Patrick, make sure the SOCOs take this for forensic analysis."

Willis noticed the lacy lingerie that was lying on the floor nearby. He stared, then took a deep breath.

"And take these, er, bits as well. And the bedding."

"Do you have any more questions for me, Inspector Willis?" Maggie asked quite calmly.

"Yes. Given the state of your dress. I'd like you to be examined by a doctor. To have a rape kit run. PC Owens is waiting to take you to the hospital."

Maggie didn't blink.

"No, Detective Inspector Willis. I will not consent to an examination. I don't believe I am obliged to. Am I?" she asked William.

"No. You are not."

"Well, then. Is there anything else?"

"No. Not at this time. But stay in the house, please." Willis sounded exasperated.

Maggie left with William. She knew Willis thought it was Bielke who had attacked her. Possibly even raped her. And she thought it was better that he believed that than found out what had actually happened.

Back in her study, William closed the door and turned to Maggie.

"Maggie. That dress. It was in shreds. Did Bielke…"

Maggie held up her hand.

"William, I know anything I say to you is confidential. And you can think what you like. But I am simply not going to discuss this. With you. With Willis. With anyone. Not now. Not ever."

"But…"

"No. Now, let's try to figure out who really did kill that vile man."

Susan Alexander

Chapter 24

Willis was back in the library. Everyone had been questioned. Few had had alibis. But no one seemed to have had a motive to kill Bielke either. And while some of the Swedes had been guarded during their interviews, he had not determined that any had been victims of Bielke's blackmailing. A couple of the women were nervous, but that was to be expected, under the circumstances.

And then there was the language issue. He could not be sure if some of the answers he had received reflected a limited command of English. And he certainly didn't know any Swedish. He wondered if he should call in a translator, but that could take days. Especially with the Christmas holidays.

The grandmother—Willis thought of her as the grandmother because he was working off the list Maggie had provided—was a dragon. But to his surprise, helpful.

"Can you tell me where you were between ten o'clock and noon?"

Ulrika von Fersen looked at Willis like he was an idiot.

"Surely you are aware we were all out until nearly noon. Then in our rooms. Then in the dining room for lunch."

"All of you?"

"All of my family except Bielke. Who was not actually family, thankfully."

"Why do you say thankfully?"

"Because he was what you British would call a scoundrel."

"A scoundrel? What do you mean by that?"

Ulrika debated what she was going to say.

"I suppose you should know. Bielke… he would pursue women. A woman. It didn't matter if she were married or not. Sometimes whether she wanted his attentions or not. Like with…" She paused.

"Yes, Mrs von Fersen?"

She pressed her lips together.

"Like with Lady Raynham?"

She shrugged.

"And was he successful? In his pursuits?"

"Surprisingly often. He would go after women of… a certain age. Whose marriages had become stale. Passionless. Who were unhappy because they saw their beauty giving way to age. They would be flattered by his attentions. He was a distinguished man. Sophisticated. Charming. And I cannot deny he was attractive."

"Do you know any of these women that he was, er, successful with? Anyone here, for instance?"

Ulrika shrugged again.

"But surely Lady Raynham is not one of those women. She is only recently married. Accomplished. Still beau…"

Willis stopped abruptly as Ulrika von Fersen regarded him with sudden interest.

"Maybe you are right. But there was no one else here with whom Bielke could… play his game. Perhaps he saw her as a challenge."

Willis considered this. Trueblood-Fitch had said something similar.

"Would it surprise you to know Bielke was a blackmailer?"

"A blackmailer? Really?"

Willis could see the woman was thinking about this.

"Do you know anyone he might have been blackmailing, Mrs von Fersen?"

"You think I am as indiscrete as some of Bielke's women? I have no direct knowledge. Only observations. And I don't repeat gossip. You are the detective, so I suggest you observe as well. And detect."

"Who do you think murdered Mr Bielke?"

"I have no idea. But even without the blackmail, I assume there are women who were unhappy when their affairs ended. And their husbands, if they found out."

"And are any of those women, and husbands, here, Mrs von Fersen?"

"You are the detective, Inspector. I suggest you ask," she repeated.

Willis glared at Ulrika von Fersen. She glared back. Finally she stood.

"And now I have answered your questions. I am not sad the man is dead, but I assure you I did not kill that…"

Ulrika used some Swedish terms. Willis assumed he could guess what they meant.

Leaning on her cane, Ulrika von Fersen left.

Patrick sprang up to open the door for the matriarch. He closed it and he and Willis looked at each other.

"Well, I guess she told us," Willis said.

"It does seem like Bielke may have, um, had an affair with one of the other Swedes."

"Yes. But which one, Patrick?"

"We can ask them, can't we, sir?"

"But would they tell the truth?"

""Well, maybe we could tell if they're lying, then."

"Yes, they can't all be as good as Lady Raynham. But they're a tight bunch, these von Fersens. And that woman, she knows more than she's telling, I'm sure."

"We can always question her again. Threaten her with obstructing an investigation."

"I'm not sure that woman would be impressed with our threats, Patrick."

"You may be right, sir."

"Anyway, let's talk to the sister. She may know something."

Anna Sofia von Fersen had obviously been crying and she clutched a soggy handkerchief.

"I'm sorry for your loss, Mrs von Fersen," Willis began.

Anna Sofia nodded. "My poor Franz. So handsome. So talented. He was a great man, Inspector. He was honoured several times for his services to our country. By King Carl Gustaf himself. Who could have killed him? Killed such a wonderful man?"

Willis tried to hide his scepticism about this alternative view of his victim.

"That's what we're trying to find out, Mrs von Fersen. Do you have any ideas?"

"No. There were those who were jealous, certainly. But jealous enough to kill…" She shook her head.

"Jealous. Yes. We've been told that your brother, er, liked the ladies."

"Women. Yes. Poor Franz was always being pursued. He would complain to me. They would not leave him alone."

"Really?"

Anna Sofia nodded.

"Well, that might cause some bad feelings. Do you know anyone he, er, rejected?"

"Well, there are his ex-wives. Horrible women. Vultures."

"Ex-wives?"

"Yes. There were three."

"But are any of them here?"

"No."

"So it is unlikely one of them murdered him."

"You think the murderer is someone here?"

"Well, yes."

"Someone here in this house?"

"Yes."

"Not some intruder? Some thief?"

"No."

Willis watched Anna Sofia consider this.

"That woman, then. It must be her."

"Who do you mean, Mrs von Fersen?"

"That woman. Who is Lady Raynham."

"Why do you say that, Mrs von Fersen?"

"Constance. My Nils' new wife. She told us. The woman is a fortune hunter. She married Lord Raynham for his money. And his position."

Willis had reason to know Maggie's financial situation. And knew that she certainly did not need Raynham's money. Assuming his lordship actually had very much. Willis knew how these estates could be tied up. And how much they cost to maintain. He also knew how much Maggie disliked being called Lady Raynham. At least when her husband was not around.

He also considered Constance Conyers, now Constance von Fersen. Did she dislike Maggie so much that she would say such things to the von Fersens? Willis wondered just how much she might hate her father's new wife. Enough to frame her for murder? Willis had not seriously considered Constance as a suspect, but perhaps he should.

He turned his attention back to Anna Sofia.

"Yes. But why would that give Lady Raynham a reason to kill your brother?"

"She was pursuing him. Throwing herself at him. She was always around. Trying to get his attention."

"And what was your brother's reaction?"

"He was polite, of course. He was a gentleman. And a guest. He did not want to make unpleasantness with the wedding."

"And so…"

"So she killed him because he rejected her."

"You think so?"

"You know. Americans. Such a violent people."

It was Willis' experience that no nationality had a monopoly on violence, but he let that pass. He was also reminded of a movie one of his early girlfriends had dragged him to. Some foreign film. Japanese. With subtitles. Willis hated subtitles. But the film, what was it called? Anyhow he remembered that there was a crime but everyone involved gave a completely different version of events. He felt like Anna Sofia was certainly providing a different version of events than Maggie. Or that reporter, Trueblood-Fitch. Or Anna Sofia's mother-in-law.

"I need to ask you, Mrs von Fersen. It has been suggested that your brother was a blackmailer. That he seduced women and then blackmailed them to keep the affair a secret. Do you know anything about this?"

Anna Sofia looked horrified. "My Franz a blackmailer? No! Who would say such a thing? Was it that woman? That horrible, lying woman?"

She collapsed and began to sob hysterically.

Willis and Patrick exchanged glances. Willis nodded.

Patrick went to the door and summoned PC Owens.

"Mrs von Fersen needs to rest," Patrick said. PC Owens led the weeping woman from the room.

"And now I think it would be a good idea to have Mrs von Fersen—the newest Mrs von Fersen, our Constance—in again, Jack," he said.

Patrick left and returned with Constance.

"Please sit down, Mrs von Fersen," Willis began.

Constance looked over her shoulder, then realised Willis had been speaking to her.

"Oh. Sorry. I'm not used…"

"Yes. I can imagine. And congratulations on your marriage. I'm afraid I should have said earlier…."

"Thank you."

"A terrible thing to happen."

Constance nodded.

Willis paused. Thought about how to proceed. Came to a decision.

"When we spoke earlier, I was mainly interested in establishing people's whereabouts. During the time when Bielke… Ambassador Bielke was killed. However, during the course of our interviews, we have received some information. I thought you might be able to help."

"Anything I can do. Of course."

"What is your opinion of Lady Raynham?"

At first Constance looked blank. Then she realised to whom Willis was referring. Her expression hardened.

"Oh. You mean her."

"Yes."

Constance's eyes narrowed.

"She was having an affair with him, you know."

"With…"

"With Uncle Franz. Bielke. She didn't even try to be discrete. Nils' family was embarrassed. Uncle Franz has always had, I mean had always had a, a weakness for women. She used that. I think she did it to try to ruin my wedding. She's always resented me. She can't stand not being the centre of attention. Of having it be seen that this is really my home, not hers."

"Really?"

Constance nodded.

"Have you ever seen the painting in my father's study? The Rossetti?"

"Er, no."

"Take a look. It explains a lot. My father thought he was marrying some idealised woman in a painting he looked at every day. Instead he got… her."

Willis made a note.

"So you say Lady Raynham was having an affair with Ambassador Bielke. What was Lord Raynham's—your father's—reaction. Did he know?"

"Well, it would have been hard not to know. We all saw it, certainly."

"And his reaction was?"

"I think he did not want to do anything that would have, um, created a scene. Before the wedding."

"The wedding was yesterday morning."

"Yes."

"So what about after the wedding?"

"After?"

"Yes. Ambassador Bielke wasn't killed until twenty-four hours—a whole day—after the wedding."

Constance frowned.

"Well, there was the wedding lunch. And the ball last night. My father would never have done anything to ruin those things for me."

"So that leaves this morning as the earliest time your father could have confronted Bielke."

"Well, yes. But…."

Constance frowned.

"What are you implying, Inspector?"

"Me? Nothing. As I recall, I simply asked what your father's reaction was to his wife's having an affair with Bielke. And you said he would not have done anything to spoil things for you."

"No. Of course not. He would never…."

"So you think your father waited until this morning to kill Bielke?"

Constance looked horrified.

"No! I never said that! You're distorting my words!"

"You don't think your father killed Bielke?"

"Of course he didn't. He would never… She's the one. She's the one who did it."

"Lady Raynham killed Bielke?"

"Yes. She's shot people before, you know."

"But why would Lady Raynham kill her lover?"

"Maybe… Maybe she wanted to run off with him and he refused. Maybe he wanted to end the affair. Maybe he rejected her."

"But why would Lady Raynham want to go off with the Ambassador? He has no title. Or wealth. If, as you say, that's the reason she married your father."

"How would I know?" Constance snapped.

"But you just said Lady Raynham was the one who murdered Bielke. Not your father. I'm simply curious as to why you would think so."

"Because of who she is. Because it's what she would do. Not my father. My father would never do something like that."

"I see. Do you have any concrete evidence for your views?"

"No. I just know."

Constance thought.

"Wait. I did see her going into the gardens. From my bedroom window. When I was getting ready for lunch. And she was carrying something. In her hand. It looked like she had a gun."

"What time was this?"

"I'm not exactly sure. Around noon, maybe."

"Around the time when Lady Raynham says she found Bielke, you mean."

"Well, maybe she didn't just find him. Maybe she shot him first. And then pretended she'd found him."

Willis congratulated himself that he had made no mention of how Bielke was actually killed to anyone at Beaumatin. And apparently neither of the Raynhams had said anything either.

"Did anyone else see Lady Raynham, do you know? Your husband, perhaps?"

"Nils?" Constance thought. "No. I think he was in the bathroom."

"I see." Willis made a note.

"Well, thank you, Mrs von Fersen."

"It's Doctor von Fersen."

"My apologies. Dr von Fersen."

Willis stood, followed by Constance.

"So are you going to arrest her?" she asked eagerly.

Willis and Patrick exchanged glances.

"Not just yet," Willis finally said.

"Oh."

Constance's disappointment was obvious.

Patrick opened the door for her and then closed it.

Willis shook his head.

"She really hates Lady Raynham, doesn't she?" Patrick said.

"Yes, she does."

"But does she hate her enough to kill someone and try to make it look like Lady Raynham did it?"

"Unlikely. I don't see her using that trowel, do you? And she obviously seems to think Bielke was shot. But if she had a chance to throw suspicion? To frame Lady Raynham? I wouldn't put it past her. Now if Lady Raynham were the victim…"

"We'd know where to look, wouldn't we, sir," Patrick.

"Yes, we would. In the meantime, how about you see about some tea."

The sergeant left while Willis sat back down and thought. He had been shocked by Constance's undisguised hatred of Maggie. What had Maggie done to make the girl feel that way? Possibly nothing, beyond marrying her father.

Willis acknowledged to himself that he was in danger of letting his personal feelings affect his objectivity. Was he discounting Maggie as a suspect because of Constance's venom? And choosing to focus on Raynham because of his dislike of the man?

DS Patrick returned with two mugs of tea, provided by a frazzled Mrs Cook. Jack Patrick was a rising star in the Gloucestershire CID and had been assigned to their best detective. He had been finishing his first year of university when his father had died unexpectedly and he had returned home to Cirencester to help support his mother and four younger siblings. He had joined the constabulary in a spirit of romance fed by TV police dramas. While most of his illusions had subsequently been shattered, he was nonetheless finding the work interesting.

He looked at his superior, who had his eyes closed and was massaging his forehead.

"You know what this reminds me of, sir?" Patrick said.

Willis opened his eyes, asked "What?" and then closed them again.

"Othello. You know? That play by Shakespeare?"

Patrick had been studying English literature.

Willis sat up and took a sip of his tea.

"Vaguely. Remind me."

"Well. Othello is this famous general. He's black, which was a much bigger deal back then than it would be now. Because he's married Desdemona, a socially prominent white girl. Usually she's played by a blonde, just to emphasize the racial difference."

"And her being blonde is what reminds you…"

"Uh. No. Sorry. Anyhow, Othello has made an enemy of Iago because he promoted this other guy over him. So Iago, who's a real bad 'un, wants revenge. It gets complicated but basically Iago makes Othello think Desdemona has gotten involved with the other guy and plants a handkerchief Othello had given Desdemona in the other guy's rooms as proof. Othello goes crazy and strangles Desdemona, then kills himself. What you'd expect to happen in Shakespeare. Lots of bodies."

"So you think the Raynhams are Othello and Desdemona? Does that make Bielke Iago? But he was murdered. Or is the murderer your Iago?"

"I couldn't say, sir. And I guess it's not completely similar. But for the jealousy. And the suspicion. And Bielke trying to make Raynham think he was having an affair with his wife. Kind of like Iago. And we're still not sure if he might've been or not. Or if he even might have raped her. But even if she's innocent, if Raynham thinks she's guilty…"

"You think she might be in danger?"

"I'm not sure, sir. But jealousy. It's a powerful motive for murder, isn't it?"

Patrick left and Willis looked down at the pictures Knowles had taken that were spread out on the table. One had caught Maggie dancing with Bielke while Raynham watched. Maggie's face was frozen, while Bielke's expression was that of a cat playing with a mouse.

Maggie was wearing that dress. Before it had been ripped and torn. Willis looked at the picture and thought Maggie in that dress alone could drive a man to murder. And in the background, Raynham was staring at the two dancers, his mouth a thin line and his eyes hard.

The second picture showed Maggie and Raynham dancing. Knowles had caught them mid-whirl and Maggie's skirt billowed behind her. That dress again. Maggie had the frozen expression it had had with Bielke. Raynham's expression was harsh. Implacable.

The final picture had caught Maggie and Raynham standing together on the side of the dance floor. Maggie was watching the dancers. Her unhappiness was obvious. She wasn't aware that her husband was looking at her. Willis stared.

The detective had never seen a murder actually committed. By the time he got to a crime scene, the only thing there was a body. Sometimes the perpetrator was there as well, if it were a case of a bar fight. Or domestic violence. But it was always after the fact.

But Raynham's expression. Willis wondered again if Patrick was right and Maggie could be in danger. Because there was only one word to describe the look on Raynham's face. Murderous.

Chapter 25

Patrick interrupted Willis' unpleasant thoughts.

"The SOCOs have found something, sir. In fact, a couple of things. They said you should come."

Willis followed Patrick to the area adjacent to where Bielke's body had been found. He was relieved that the rain had finally let up.

"We found these, sir. Hidden behind that bush there," the SOCO explained.

Willis looked at a blood-soaked jacket and a pair of gardening gloves that were equally bloody.

"All right. Bag them. And let me have the weapon, the trowel, as well. We'll see if anyone can identify them. It's a man's jacket. We'll start with Raynham."

"And that's not all, sir," the SOCO continued. "This was in Lady Raynham's pants pocket."

The SOCO showed Willis a plastic bag that held a pistol. A .22.

Willis stared at the gun.

"And it's been fired, sir. Recently. Three times."

"Fingerprints?"

"One set, sir. We won't be sure whose they are until we check."

"Make it a priority, then. And let me know as soon as you've identified the prints. Although for now I'll assume they're Mag... Lady Raynham's."

"That seems reasonable, sir. Given they were in her pants pocket."

"So give me the gun as well. I'll see what Lady Raynham has to say for herself. And you need to check her for gunshot residue. And her clothes."

He turned to Patrick. "And tell the pathologist to check to make sure that Bielke wasn't shot before he was, er, troweled. Maybe using the trowel was an attempt to cover up a shooting."

Patrick went off to carry out Willis' orders. Eventually he summoned Thomas and William to the library, where Willis was waiting.

When everyone was seated, the detective said, "Lord Raynham. These were found in your garden. We hope you can be helpful in identifying them. Patrick?"

The sergeant held up the bloody jacket with gloved hands.

"That's a shooting jacket," said Thomas indifferently.

"Yes. Have you ever seen it before?"

Thomas shrugged.

"Lord Raynham?" Willis pressed.

"Certainly not in its current state."

"In any state," Willis was becoming annoyed by Thomas' attitude.

"I'd have to look…"

Thomas got up.

"Patrick."

"I need to see the label."

Patrick held the jacket open for Thomas.

Thomas glanced at William and sat back down.

"Yes. That's mine."

"I see. And these?"

Patrick showed Thomas the gardening gloves.

"They're gardening gloves."

"Yes. That much is obvious. But do you recognise them?"

"We must have one, two dozen pairs of gloves like these here. Or ones that are similar to these."

"Very well. And what about this?"

Patrick showed him the trowel.

"Same thing. We must have six, eight…"

"Let's return to the jacket then. You say it's yours?"

"Yes."

"When was the last time you wore it."

"Possibly the day before yesterday. Or the day before that. Not yesterday. The day of the wedding. Otherwise I can't say for certain."

"Where do you keep it?"

"A room off the kitchen. With other jackets. Boots. Hats. Scarves. Umbrellas. Even trowels and gardening gloves. Anyone could have taken it."

"Anyone?"

Thomas shrugged.

"And when were you last in your garden again?"

"This morning. No, it was early afternoon in fact. When Mag… Lady Raynham told me she'd found Ambassador Bielke's body. I went to see…"

"What were you wearing?"

Thomas thought.

"What I have on now."

"It was raining. You didn't want a jacket? Boots?"

"I was told there had been a murder. I went right out."

"In the rain?"

Thomas gestured irritably.

"And those were the shoes you were wearing?"

Thomas looked down at his brogues.

"Yes."

"We'd like to take them, please. To compare them with the footprints we've found."

Thomas looked annoyed.

"It's routine procedure, Lord Raynham," Willis said reasonably.

"Very well. I'll change and…"

"We'd prefer that you gave them to us now," Willis said.

Thomas glanced at William who indicated his father should do as he was asked.

Thomas untied his shoes and reluctantly handed them to Patrick.

"Thank you."

Apparently his lordship was not used to walking around his home in his socks, Willis concluded. Too bad.

There was a pause. Then Thomas said, "If I might ask. Where did you find those?"

"The jacket and gloves, you mean?"

"Yes."

Willis thought and decided there was no harm in answering.

"Behind some sort of bush. In an area adjacent to where the body was found."

"I see."

Thomas thought.

"Well, Inspector Willis, if, as I suspect, you believe that I was the one wearing that jacket and those gloves when I murdered Bielke, there are other places I could have disposed of them that you would not have found so easily. Or at all."

"Perhaps. Although in my experience, people's actions after they've committed a murder are often mindless. Irrational. Or perhaps you saw Lady Raynham approaching and had to conceal them as best you could at the moment."

"I saw no one. As I was not there."

"Yes. Lady Raynham was emphatic that she did not see you in the garden. In fact, she did her best to convince me that she had killed Bielke."

Thomas was startled.

"Why would Ma… that woman kill her lover? It certainly wasn't to keep the affair from becoming known. They were hardly being discrete."

"Why indeed? It seems much more likely to me that a jealous husband, wearing his own jacket and out doing some garden chore, was provoked into murdering his rival. He could even claim to have acted on impulse. Except for that second blow. The one which drove the trowel up into Bielke's heart. That was no impulse."

Thomas was about reply when William put his hand on his arm to silence him.

Disappointed not to have provoked a reaction, Willis continued.

"But what I find most hard to understand in all this is your attitude, Lord Raynham. After all, isn't this just a case of, what's sauce for the goose is sauce for the gander? Or have you already forgotten Natalie Perkins?"

Thomas sat as though turned to stone. William stood and touched his father's shoulder to indicate that he should follow.

"I believe this interview is over, Detective Inspector," William said.

"For now," agreed Willis.

After father and son left, Willis said to Patrick, "Let's talk to Lady Raynham. I want to see what she has to say about that jacket. And the gun."

Maggie had shut herself in her study to avoid the von Fersens.

"Detective Inspector Willis would like to see you, Lady Raynham."

It was young Patrick.

"Very well," she said, while she wondered, "What now?"

"You wanted to see me, Inspector Willis?"

"Yes. I wanted to ask if you recognised this. Patrick?"

Patrick held up the bag with the gun.

Maggie looked. "It's a gun."

Willis suppressed a sigh.

"Yes. Obviously it's a gun."

"Well, what did you expect me to say?" Maggie asked reasonably.

"Patrick. Show her," said the exasperated detective.

Patrick brought the bag with its contents over to Maggie.

"It looks like a .22." She paused. "Oh."

"Oh, what?"

"Um. Where did you find this?"

"I expect that is something you might be able to tell us. And explain."

"Oh. Oh dear. Well…"

Maggie looked embarrassed. Sighed.

"You found it in my pants pocket, didn't you? When I gave my clothes to PC Owens. I forgot that it was there. With the, er, shock of finding Bielke."

"A bit careless, were you?"

Maggie gave a brief laugh.

"Apparently," she finally said.

"And why were you carrying a gun?"

Maggie thought about what she should say. Willis watched her.

"The truth, please."

"I had threatened to shoot Bielke. If he persisted in his… behaviour. Towards me. As I am not in the habit of making idle threats…" she shrugged.

"And for how long had you had the gun with you?"

"Since... After Bielke's visit this morning. I took it from the gun room before I went out. Into the gardens."

Willis stared at Maggie without expression. She stared back calmly. Was she telling the truth? He had no idea.

"The gun has been fired recently. And when the SOCO tested your jacket just now, it was positive for gunshot residue. Would you care to explain that?"

Maggie was silent for a moment. Then she said, "I was upset about... About everything. I was walking in the gardens. I took a few shots. To calm down. Better to shoot at a tree than..."

She paused.

"Anyhow I can probably find the tree for you. At least I think I can. I could try, anyway. Would you like me to..."

Willis held up his hand.

"Not right now. So you're saying I don't need to tell the pathologist he should make sure Bielke wasn't shot before he was... trowelled?" he asked,

Maggie said nothing while she thought. Finally she shook her head.

"All right. Next, Patrick."

Patrick reached down and picked up the jacket. He held it up.

Maggie looked at the jacket for a long moment. Then she looked back at Willis.

"It's a shooting jacket."

"Yes. We know that."

"And it's covered in blood."

"Yes. We see that as well. But my question is, do you know whose it is?"

"All shooting jackets look very much alike to me, Inspector."

"Perhaps if you take a closer look. Patrick?"

Maggie stared at the jacket. And its label. Finally she said, "It is possible that it is Lord Raynham's."

"Yes. He confirmed that it was his."

"Then why did you…"

Willis stared at her. She stared back.

"Do you still hold to your earlier statement that you did not see Lord Raynham in the garden?"

"Yes. Yes I do. He wasn't there."

"Do you know where he was, if he wasn't in the garden?"

"Well, I can't say with absolute certainty. As I told you, Bielke said Thomas was out with Ned. Ned Thatcher. I am sure he can confirm that. I don't know when Thomas returned, but when I saw him in the hall he was no longer wearing his riding clothes, so I suppose he must have changed. It's a routine he has. When he comes back from a ride, he showers and puts on fresh clothes. Normally he would then work in his study. Until lunch."

"So tell me, Lady Raynham..."

She held up a hand.

"Please. It's still Maggie. Especially since..." She paused.

"Very well. Maggie. How do you suppose all this blood came to be on Lord Raynham's jacket?"

"But you can't use my... suppositions as evidence."

"No. But I'd be interested to know your opinion."

"All right. Well, the jacket. It's kept in a room off the kitchen. With other jackets. Boots. Hats. In the US, we'd call it a mud room.

"The room is open. In fact our guests had gotten into the habit of using the boots and jackets and hats that are there. I don't think they were prepared for how muddy the grounds are. Or for the wet weather we're having, for that matter. So anyone could have borrowed it. Taken it. It was raining. And the person wouldn't necessarily have known it was Thomas'."

"So you don't think the murderer was trying to incriminate Thomas?"

Maggie thought. Finally she said, "That would assume whoever was wearing that jacket knew in advance that he—or she—was going to murder Bielke. And was going to try to incriminate Thomas."

"You don't think the murder was premeditated then?"

"Inspector, in your experience, does anyone plan to kill someone with a garden trowel?"

Willis frowned. He had to admit, she had a point.

"In fact, when I told Thomas I had found Bielke and that he was dead, Thomas immediately assumed I had been the one who had killed him. That I had accidentally shot him. And certainly if someone were planning to murder Bielke, well, as you know, the gun room is not kept locked. Even if the cabinets are. And a group of us were out shooting just a few days ago."

Willis thought about this. He continued.

"So someone went out to the garden with a trowel. It was raining so they took a jacket. This jacket. Lord Raynham's jacket. The person was either following Bielke or Bielke was following him."

"Or her."

"Or her. I say following because it would be quite a coincidence for both Bielke and the murderer to be in what is a rather distant part of your garden by happenstance, don't you think?"

"I agree."

"There is a confrontation and Bielke is killed. With the trowel. By someone wearing Lord Raynham's jacket."

"Yes."

"So if this is your basic scenario, one must ask who would be most likely to be out in the garden with a trowel in the rain. Certainly not one of your houseguests.

"It seems to me the most obvious person to be out in the garden with a trowel and wearing that jacket is Lord Raynham. Bielke could have seen your husband leaving the house and followed him. Perhaps because, since you say you had told him to 'go to hell,' he was going to put his threat into effect by making sure your husband believed you were indeed having an affair.

"But Bielke goads your husband too far. He snaps and attacks Bielke with the trowel. His jacket is covered in blood. He hides it behind a bush, intending to retrieve it later. But you discover Bielke's body and call the police and he never gets the chance."

Maggie was silent. Willis could see she was thinking.

Finally she said, "That is certainly one scenario. But it is just one. Lord Raynham is not the only person to go into the gardens. In fact. I was in that exact same spot myself recently. With a trowel.

"And anyone could have taken that jacket. Since it was raining. Did you check to see whose clothes might be wet? And whose shoes are muddy? In addition to looking for blood?"

Willis frowned. The SOCOs had only searched for clothes that showed traces of blood. And it was too late now. The clothes would have dried in the meantime.

Maggie stood.

"Detective Inspector Willis, Thomas did not kill Franz Bielke."

"And just how can you be so sure?"

"Because Thomas is not a murderer. And if he were, Bielke would not be the one who is dead," she said sadly.

"Then who…"

But Maggie had left.

Susan Alexander

Chapter 26

It was Christmas Eve day. Grey. Drizzly. Not very Christmas-like, despite the huge tree in the dining room and the forest of pines in the great hall hung with Derek's and Damien's fairy lights.

Maggie knew what the plan had been. A leisurely day with an early family dinner. Festive. For the children. James Conyers' were still at William's. She had gotten all the children gifts. She had enjoyed that. A ship for young Thomas. A blonde Madame Alexander doll for Elizabeth. A train set for Harry. And an elaborate wooden block set for John.

But what would happen now? She did not want the children's Christmas spoiled by the death of a bad man they did not even know. Perhaps she could drive over to William's and deliver the presents herself. Leave them with Gweneth. She didn't think that Willis would object. As long as she was still in Gloucestershire.

She had gotten some coffee from Mrs Cook and was returning when she heard voices coming from Thomas' study. Well, he would certainly know what was happening. Or could make a decision. Just because he was being an idiot didn't mean she should act like one too. She needed to talk to him.

She tapped on the door, then pushed it open. Thomas was there. And William.

"Oh good. I'm glad you're both here," she began in as normal a tone as possible.

Thomas scowled. He stood up.

"You!"

"Thomas?"

"It's bad enough having to have you in my house. I won't have you barging in here…"

"Father!" William was shocked.

Thomas rushed at Maggie to thrust her out of the room. She tried to avoid him, staggered, tripped and went crashing down. The mug tipped and spilled coffee all over. Off balance, Thomas fell on top of her.

"Oh. No. Don't."

Maggie was struggling to disentangle herself.

"Father!"

"That's enough! Stop that right now!"

Maggie knew that voice.

Suddenly Thomas was grabbed and lifted. Held. It was Sergeant Patrick.

Willis knelt down beside Maggie.

"Are you all right?"

She nodded but her eyes were filled with tears. Her clothes were soaked with coffee.

Willis stood. He helped her up. He had been haunted all night by the picture of Raynham, looking murderous. And now this. He felt he couldn't take any further chances.

"Lord Raynham, you're under arrest for the murder of Franz Bielke. And for assaulting Lady Raynham. Patrick."

Sergeant Patrick tried to hide his surprise. This had not been planned. On the other hand, he had seen the man attacking his wife with his own eyes.

Patrick repeated the caution, nodded at the two constables. One put Thomas in handcuffs.

Maggie put her hand on Willis' arm.

"Inspector Willis? Please. Listen to me. You're making a mistake. Thomas wasn't…" Maggie was desperate.

Willis was expressionless. Avoiding her eyes, he gently removed Maggie's hand, turned and went out.

For a frantic moment, Maggie thought that, to spare Thomas, she should go after Willis and confess to the murder herself.

"But that would be the act of a lesser woman. And I am not a lesser woman," she reminded herself. It would also be stupid, as she doubted Willis would believe her.

Instead she said, "William?"

"I'll follow them," he said.

The von Fersens had been having breakfast in the dining room. The commotion had brought them all into the hall.

Anna Sofia von Fersen saw Thomas in handcuffs, guarded by the constables, and shrieked, "It was you! You killed him! You killed Franz!" before she collapsed weeping on the floor.

Ulrika looked at her daughter-in-law with contempt.

"Do something, Georg Axel. Get her out of here," the matriarch said to her son.

George Axel helped his sobbing wife get up and led her into the drawing room.

Constance rushed up to Maggie.

"You! This is all your fault! I knew you'd ruin everything! I hate you!"

She started to cry.

"Constance! Stop that right now!"

Maggie thought William sounded just like his father.

"Nils, would you please…" William asked.

Nils pulled himself together, put his arm around his new wife and led her back to the kitchen.

The rest of the von Fersen family stood awkwardly, like witnesses to a bad accident. They knew they should leave but were mesmerized by the horror of it all.

Damien and Derek emerged from the ballroom they were still de-decorating after the previous day's interruptions. They came and stood by Maggie.

"Don't worry, Maggie," said Derek and put his arm around her.

Damien saw Knowles taking pictures. He rushed over and wrenched the camera from the photographer's hand.

"No you don't."

"But Mr Lionel…" Knowles whined and pointed upwards.

Lionel Trueblood-Fitch was standing on the landing and observing the drama below. Damien saw him turn away, but not in time to hide a smirk.

Maggie watched the police constables take Thomas out. He stared straight ahead, his face a frozen mask. Willis and Patrick followed.

William addressed the remaining von Fersens.

"This is all a mistake. Police over-zealousness. I need to go accompany my father. Please make yourselves as comfortable as possible until I return. If there is anything you require, I am sure Lady Raynham or Mrs Cook…" he gestured. The housekeeper had also come into the hall and was looking as though her world had just collapsed around her,

The von Fersens slowly moved back into the dining room.

William came over to where Maggie was standing with Derek and Damien.

"I must go. You'll be all right?"

Maggie nodded.

"I need to deal with the arrest. I'm certain there's not enough evidence…"

William tried to sound more confident than he felt.

"And when he's released, I promise I will personally knock some sense into his thick head."

Maggie tried to smile.

"Thank you. Please let me know…"

"I will keep you informed."

William left.

"Time for a council of war," Damien said.

"My study?"

"Yes. Derek, could you ask Mrs Cook for some tea? And coffee for Maggie, of course," Damien said.

"That's all right. Damien. I'll go. I think Mrs Cook needs a bit of comforting."

Maggie returned a few minutes later with Mrs Cook bearing a tray with tea and coffee.

"And perhaps ask the von Fersens if they would like something as well.

Mrs Cook nodded glumly and left.

"Well!" Derek was agitated.

"Where do we stand on our investigation?" asked Damien.

"The murderer must be pleased that Thomas was arrested. Perhaps he… and I do think it's a he… will be off guard."

"Er, Maggie. You don't think it's at all possible that Thomas…" Derek asked hesitantly.

"No. Thomas is not a murderer," Maggie said firmly.

"Okay. Well, you were right about that before. So. Moving on," said Derek.

"Yes. So. What do we know?"

"Well we do know some things. More than we did when we last talked," said Damien.

"Tell her, Day."

"First, I talked to Elisabeth. And she told me about her and Bielke."

"So there was something?" Maggie asked.

"Oh my, yes," said Derek.

"Bielke tried the same thing with Elisabeth as he was trying with you. With more success. Well, if I were married to Carl Magnus, I might be susceptible too. Bor-ing.

"Anyhow, Bielke seduced Elisabeth. They had a brief affair. Then one day he tells her he wants money or he'll tell Carl Magnus. And he had pictures. That was two years ago. So far she's paid him around £25,000 if my currency conversion is correct. And she still doesn't have the pictures. Or know if he made copies."

"That's why, when you'd think she'd be singing the Hallelujah Chorus because Bielke is dead, she looks even more worried. She's afraid of those pictures turning up," Derek said.

"You don't think he'd have them here, would he?" Maggie asked.

Damien shrugged. "No idea. And the police have sealed his room, so trying to get in to look would be difficult."

"But speaking of getting into people's rooms," said Derek.

"Oh yes. Well, Derek nobly offered to take one for the team," Damien continued.

"He spent yesterday evening with Trueblood-Fitch. Who was only too happy to help him de-decorate the ballroom. Holding the ladder and gazing up at his sweet little bum."

"And patting it too," Derek reminded his partner.

"And patting it too," Damien agreed. "Thank goodness we didn't hang up any mistletoe."

"Anyway, he suggested we retire to this little inn he knew in the neighbourhood for… well, you can imagine.

"I said sorry, but I had to be true to my Damien," Derek continued.

"And he said, 'If I were twenty years younger, I'd have you!'"

"And I said…"

"Not if you were thirty years younger!" Derek and Damien chorused together.

"I mean, really. What was he thinking?" Derek finished.

Maggie shook her head. Damien continued.

"Meanwhile, I went to see Mrs Cook. I told her you had told us about the missing objects. And said you had asked me to check Trueblood-Fitch's room while he was being distracted by Derek. She was happy to tell me where it was. In your old servant's wing, I gather. And how to get there. She nearly had to draw me a map."

Maggie was not surprised. She had yet to visit the servants' wing. As well as other parts of the house.

"Anyhow, I snuck up. Knowles was out at some pub, Mrs Cook thought. And I found your objets d'art. Those two hideous doggies and a nice little snuff box and that dagger were wrapped in some socks in a dresser drawer."

"Did you take them?"

"No. I thought I should talk to you before I did that. Because then Trueblood-Fitch would know he'd been rumbled and might do a runner."

"That's true. I'd ask if there were any blood-stained trousers or shirts but I guess the police would have taken them."

"No. Because Mrs Cook said the police hadn't looked in the servants' wing. They concentrated on the guests' rooms. And yours and Raynham's. She didn't think they even knew there was a servants' wing. Or that anyone was staying there. And she said it wasn't her policy to volunteer information to the police. Unless they asked. Which they hadn't."

That produced a smile from Maggie.

"But even so, I didn't find anything with blood. Or at least not in his closet. Of course, in this place. Well, there'd be lots of rooms and closets and nooks and crannies where you could hide things."

Maggie nodded.

"So Trueblood-Fitch is the thief. But does that make him the murderer? What reason would he have to kill Bielke?" Maggie wondered aloud.

Damien shrugged. Maggie continued.

"However. It does occur to me. Just like Bielke and his blackmail. Do you think this is the first time Trueblood-Fitch has helped himself to some valuables? Maybe he did the same thing at the other places where he's done stories. If I could get a list, could you make some calls? Check to see if anyone else has had things go missing? You can say you're calling on my behalf. Um, on Lady Raynham's behalf."

"Aha. So you do use your title," said Derek.

"Only when I absolutely have to," said Maggie defensively.

"No problem, Maggie."

"But before I find out about our resident rapporteur, as he likes to call himself, let's review where we are in our investigation.

"So we're eliminating you guys and myself and Thomas."

The two men exchanged glances. They did not completely share Maggie's blind faith in her husband's innocence.

"And Mrs Cook and Mrs Griggs and Mrs Bateson."

The men nodded.

"Then there's Ned and Jamie and Ian and Wesley. I'm eliminating them as well."

"Er, Maggie. You don't think, if someone were in the garden with a trowel, if might have been one of them?"

"Yes, except there's really nothing much to be done in the gardens right now. This time of year it's pretty much all sheep, all the time. And what reason would any of them have to kill Bielke?

"And they are all so loyal to Thomas. I can't believe one of them would stand by and let him be arrested. And I think Ned or Mrs Cook would notice if one of the others had done something like that. They're all good guys. I don't think any of them would hide his guilt very well."

"So we'll put them down as probably not," said Damien, who was taking notes.

"Then there's Thomas' family. But William and James and Gweneth and Victoria were at William's when Bielke was killed. And I called William there when I found the body. And he was playing with the children. So they can be eliminated. No opportunity. As well as no motive."

"And Constance and Nils?" Damien asked.

"Could Bielke have been coming on to her as well?" Derek wondered.

"Not that I noticed. And there was no tension between him and Nils. And Constance? I don't think I've ever even seen her in the gardens. She doesn't seem to be interested. So why would she be out with a trowel?"

"Could the trowel have just been left there?" Damien wondered.

"Unlikely. You've seen the gardens. A fallen leaf is hardly allowed to lie around. And I was in the same place a few days before and there was no trowel there then. And I would have seen it and picked it up."

"So Constance and Nils are Probably Nots as well."

"And I think we can eliminate Ulrika von Fersen. She's not strong enough. Although I did think a few times she would have liked to have beaten Bielke with her cane. And the same goes for Agneta. Because she's pregnant."

"You don't think pregnancy hormones…" Derek began.

"Oh really, Derek. No. Why are men so intimidated by pregnant women?"

"Because we're afraid we might suddenly be called upon to deliver a baby," Damien explained.

"Miz Scarlet. Miz Scarlet. I don't know nothin' 'bout birthin' babies," said Derek, imitating Prissy in *Gone with the Wind*.

Damien laughed and Maggie shook her head.

"So the Ekeblads' are Probably Nots as well." Damien said.

"Did Elisabeth think Bielke was blackmailing any of the other von Fersens? It might not have been sexual. Several are in the government. Georg Axel was a judge. Carl Magnus is a banker. Could one of them have done something they would pay Bielke to keep secret?" Maggie asked.

"Hmm. I didn't ask. But I think Elisabeth would have said something if she knew," Damien said.

"Well, if necessary, maybe you could talk to her again."

Damien nodded.

"So what about Elisabeth?" Maggie asked.

"I think if she were going to kill Bielke, she would have done it earlier, when the blackmail started," Damien said.

"But here at Beaumatin, she had a lot of other people around who could be possible suspects. Especially Thomas and I. Maybe she just seized an opportunity," Maggie argued.

"But if she had killed Bielke, why would she have told me he was blackmailing her? She would never have told me that if she had murdered him," countered Damien.

"That's true. And she did try to warn me," Maggie added.

"And don't forget the pictures. She would still be worried about them," Derek pointed out.

"Maybe she found the pictures. In Bielke's room. Bielke hung around down here most of the time. Because that's where I was, unfortunately. That gave her a lot of chances to look."

"Assuming he brought them with him. Wouldn't that be a strange thing to do?"

They all thought about this.

"All right. I'll put her down as a Maybe. Although personally. I doubt it," said Damien.

"What about Carl Magnus then? Supposing he found out about the affair?" Derek asked.

"Or the blackmail?" Maggie added.

She thought.

"Well, I've been with him at meals and he seemed more interested in his wine than anything else. And I was out shooting with him and Elisabeth and Bielke. Clay pigeons. Bielke was showing Elisabeth how to aim. He had his arms around her. And Carl Magnus seemed quite unperturbed." Unlike how Thomas would have reacted, she added to herself.

"And don't you think Elisabeth would know if Carl Magnus had found out?" she continued.

"All right. So we'll list Carl Magnus as a Probably Not," Damien decided.

"What about Nils' other brother. And his wife? Fredrik and Margaretha?" Maggie asked.

"Hmm. In fact, I don't think Margaretha would have been susceptible to Bielke," said Derek.

"Why not?"

"Well, to her, he would have been just a horny old fart," said Derek.

"That's true," agreed Damien.

"She's, what, late twenties? He's over sixty, I'd guess. Forty would seem old to her," explained Derek.

"Definitely not his demographic. He'd need to go for older women. Oh. Sorry Maggie."

"That's all right, Damien. In fact, I think you're right. And most younger women probably wouldn't have the money, or the jewels, to pay off Bielke. And an older woman would definitely be more vulnerable. More receptive to his advances."

"He did have a certain villainous charm," agreed Damien.

"Lucius Malfoy," said Derek.

"That's exactly what I've been thinking," said Maggie.

"So that leaves our friendly reporter. Oh. I'm sorry. Rapporteur," said Derek.

"We know he's a thief," said Damien.

"And a shameless wannabe seducer," added Derek.

"But does that make him a murderer?" Maggie asked.

"He's a bad man. I think he'd be capable of anything," said Derek.

"Consider his taste in tweed," Damien said.

"All right. But until we have some proof, he's still a maybe," Maggie insisted.

"And let's not forget Knowles," Derek said.

"Yes, master. Yes, master," said Damien, getting up and doing an Igor imitation.

"You know. I don't think I've said a single word to Knowles. I've just been reacting to him physically," Maggie reflected.

"His ferretousness," said Derek.

"Yes. Which is probably quite unfair. Since I know nothing about him as a person," said Maggie.

"Except that he works for Trueblood-Fitch. Which shows there's a problem somewhere," Derek pointed out.

"Maybe I should check his room too," said Damien.

"That's probably a good idea," Maggie agreed.

"Although I may find out he's put pictures of kittens and ducklings and daffodils up on the walls," said Damien.

"Or perhaps you'll find a pile of bloody clothes under his bed," said Derek.

"I'll let you check where his room is with Mrs Cook. Although I assume it would be next to Trueblood-Fitch's. And I'll try to get that list of other places where Trueblood-Fitch has done stories," Maggie said.

"And I'll see if I can talk to Elisabeth some more," finished Damien.

The men left.

Maggie googled Trueblood-Fitch. She found dozens of references. And at least eight stories about houses that were doubtless filled with the kind of small objects that the man would find tempting. She made a list for Derek and Damien.

Maggie sighed. She had been trying not to think about Thomas. Alone. In a cell. Believing she had been unfaithful. Blaming her for his predicament. Hating her. Thank goodness people were no longer hanged for murder. But even so, the thought of Thomas sent to prison… If it looked like that might happen, she really would confess to the murder. And make Willis believe her.

Susan Alexander

Chapter 27

It was after lunch and Maggie was in her room. Mrs Cook had brought her up a sandwich so she could continue to avoid the von Fersens. Constance could play hostess, she decided.

Her door opened and Constance burst in. Maggie could tell she had been crying.

"You can't let my father be arrested for a crime he didn't commit. You can't. You have to tell the police that it was you who shot Bielke. Please. I'm begging you."

Maggie was about to protest that she had done everything she could to prevent Thomas' arrest, when she processed what Constance had said. She thought quickly.

"But Bielke wasn't shot," Maggie told the distraught woman.

"He wasn't shot? What do you mean?"

"Bielke wasn't shot. He was killed with a garden trowel. And the police found blood all over your father's shooting jacket. Which is why Willis arrested him. And not me," she explained.

Constance frowned. "He was killed with a garden trowel? And my father's shooting jacket had blood all over it?"

"Yes. Which is why Inspector Willis arrested your father," Maggie repeated herself patiently.

"Willis thinks my father killed Bielke because you were having an affair with him." Constance spoke contemptuously.

Maggie was about to protest that there was no affair but instead said, simply, "Yes."

"But it wasn't my father. It was you. I know it was you. I saw you. And I'm going to tell the police," Constance said triumphantly.

She rushed off. Doubtless to telephone Willis.

"Thank you, Constance," Maggie thought. Perhaps Thomas would not be spending Christmas alone in a cell after all. As for herself, at this point she really didn't care. It was Thomas who was important. In fact, a solitary cell might be preferable if the alternative were a Christmas spent with the von Fersens. And Constance.

Maggie had slipped back to her study and was relieved that she hadn't met anyone. She checked emails and answered the ones wishing her a merry Christmas in kind. There would be no way for anyone to know how un-merry she was actually feeling.

She considered whether playing some Christmas music would help and decided it would probably make her feel worse.

Then she saw a police car draw up in front of the house. Inspector Willis and Sergeant Patrick emerged. She assumed they were here because of Constance.

"Well played, Maggie," she congratulated herself.

She heard low voices in the hall and footsteps go by. She waited. Twenty minutes later there was a knock on her door.

"Come in."

It was Inspector Willis and Sergeant Patrick. Behind them stood Constance, eyes full of malice and smirking.

Willis turned. "You'll need to wait outside, Dr von Fersen."

"I'll wait. Just don't believe what she says. I know her. She'll lie. But I told you the truth," Constance was insistent.

Willis closed the door.

Maggie stood. "What is this about, Inspector Willis?"

"Your step-daughter had told us previously that she had seen you from her bedroom window going into the gardens around the time of Bielke's death and that you were carrying something in your hand. She assumed it was a gun. Now, however, having thought about it, she says she recognised it was a gardening tool. A trowel, in fact.

"She also says that you were wearing a shooting jacket that looked like the one her father has. And we had neglected to ask her about your appearance when we spoke to her earlier."

"Really?" Constance was so predictable, Maggie thought.

"What do you have to say to that, Lady Raynham?" Willis challenged.

"Please, Inspector, it's Ma..." she began automatically, then stopped abruptly. And was suddenly overwhelmed by the realisation that, even if Thomas were released, if he really believed she'd been having an affair with Bielke, she was unlikely to be called Lad Raynham much longer.

Willis followed her train of thought and saw how desolate she looked. Could she have murdered Bielke to keep him from carrying out his threat to destroy her marriage?

"Constance said she saw me going into the gardens carrying a trowel and wearing Thomas' shooting jacket?"

Willis was silent. He waited.

"Well, if that's what Constance says she saw, what do you want me to say?"

Willis looked into two deep pools of green. Maggie was calm. Serene. Willis wished he knew what was going on behind her eyes. Was Maggie a murderer? Or was she trying to protect her husband? He knew people lied to protect a loved one. He had experienced this on two of his cases. But Maggie wasn't lying. She was neither confirming nor denying Constance's story.

"When we talked to Constance previously, she thought Bielke had been shot."

"That's what Thomas thought as well, when I told him Bielke was dead," Maggie pointed out.

"Did you tell Constance about the trowel? And the shooting jacket?"

"Do I need to call Mr Conyers, Inspector Willis?" Maggie avoided his question.

Willis was frustrated. He was fairly certain Maggie had given Constance the information, correctly assuming that the woman would promptly call the police and say what in fact she had said. And divert suspicion away from Raynham and onto Maggie herself.

"Are you aware that there's a charge called 'obstructing an investigation'?" he demanded.

"Is that what I'm doing? Constance has made a fairly serious accusation. Are you surprised that I'm being cautious about answering your questions?" she countered.

"Nor can I prove that I wasn't carrying a trowel and wearing Thomas' jacket when Constance saw me," she added reasonably.

Willis scowled. He was fairly sure that at this point, whatever the truth, Constance would have convinced herself that she had seen Maggie carrying a trowel and wearing that shooting jacket.

"Are you going to arrest me, Inspector Willis?" Maggie asked finally.

"No. Not at this time," he said sourly.

"Are you going to release Thomas?" she asked hopefully.

"No." He didn't add that he was keeping the baron in custody out of concern for her own safety.

"But don't leave the estate. I'll want to talk to you again once we've, er, sorted this out," he said brusquely.

After Willis and Patrick left, Maggie congratulated herself that at least now there had to be reasonable doubt. Was that a concept in the UK? She'd have to ask William. Because she was absolutely certain that Constance would swear in court that she had seen Maggie in the shooting jacket with the trowel. And there was no way Thomas would be convicted if Constance testified to that.

Well, at least that was something, Maggie thought

Susan Alexander

Chapter 28

Maggie had returned to her room. After Willis had left she realised that, while she might have managed to divert some suspicion from Thomas, she had come no closer to discovering who had murdered Bielke. Or convincing Willis that he needed to look for a suspect besides Thomas and herself.

Maggie also realised that she was utterly exhausted and needed to take a "power nap." Now she was awake and trying to justify avoiding the von Fersens for another meal. Surely Constance could play hostess for dinner. It was her party, after all, and her home, as she liked to remind Maggie.

From her bedroom window, Maggie saw Lionel Trueblood-Fitch walking towards the gardens. He was wearing the most awful tweed yet. A bright green and red plaid. A Christmas tweed. Where did he find them?

Trueblood-Fitch paused and looked over his shoulder, as though he wanted to be sure he was not being followed. Then he set off again.

"Hmm. What's he up to now?" Maggie wondered.

She raced downstairs, past a dejected Mrs Cook who was stirring a large pot of soup on one of the Agas, and out the back door.

"Now where has he gone?" Maggie wondered. She saw no one and everything was still.

She had just decided to try the place where she had found the unusual snowdrop and Bielke had been murdered, when she heard a sound. Like glass breaking. Could it be the greenhouse?

She turned around and sprinted in that direction. When she was still some yards away, she heard a "Psst!" coming from behind a large yew.

"Maggie!" A frantic whisper.

"Derek?"

Derek and Damien peeked out.

"What are you doing?"

"Trueblood-Fitch has been acting squirrelly. We followed him," explained Damien.

"He's over by the greenhouse. We don't know why," added Derek.

"Well, it's locked. He can't get in. Or I don't think he can. It's one of those locks you need a key to open either side of the door. I'm going to go see what he's up to."

"Be careful," Derek cautioned.

"Call if you need us. We'll be right here," Damien added.

Maggie continued on her way and saw Trueblood-Fitch. He had broken a pane of glass in the door and had stuck his hand through. He was trying to open the door from the inside.

Trueblood-Fitch cut himself on a piece of broken glass and swore. He was sucking on a finger when Maggie said, "Lionel?"

He jumped.

"Lady Raynham," he said nervously.

"What are you doing?"

"I saw a pane of glass was broken…"

"Because you broke it yourself."

"No, I…"

"Don't deny it. I saw you," Maggie lied.

"Well, I…"

"If you want a visit, I can arrange that."

Trueblood-Fitch gave his still-bleeding finger a last lick and stuck his hand in his pocket.

"With Lord Raynham, um, away, I didn't want to be a bother."

"So you broke a window?"

Trueblood-Fitch shrugged.

"What is it that you want that's in our greenhouse?" Maggie demanded.

Trueblood-Fitch hesitated, then came to a decision.

"It's that snowdrop. The one with that green on its outer segments. I went back to have a second look, but it was gone. Do you know what happened to it?"

"Yes. I dug it up. Poachers, you know. But it's not in the greenhouse."

""Oh? Where is it then? Did you just move it to another location? I'd be very interested in seeing it again."

"Yes, it's been moved. To someplace… safe."

Maggie thought.

"But you said you went back. Would that have been on Sunday morning, by any chance?"

Trueblood-Fitch's expression turned ugly. Behind his glasses, his grey eyes narrowed. And Maggie became aware that, even though she tended to think of Trueblood-Fitch as being a little man, because of his character, and his ridiculous tweeds, in reality he was at least an inch taller than she was and quite a few stone heavier. However, she ignored her qualms and went on.

"And could Franz Bielke have followed you? It's the sort of thing he'd do."

"That fraud. Pretending to be so superior. When he was nothing but a common criminal," Trueblood-Fitch sneered.

"Yes. He was a blackmailer."

"And he thought he could blackmail me. He was in the library. In a wing back chair. The light was dim. I didn't see him. But he saw me. I was admiring some of your little treasures. He accused me of stealing one of them and said he'd tell Raynham unless I paid him off."

"Treasures like the snuff box? And the dagger? And the Staffordshire dogs?"

"Yes. I mean, no. I mean… How do you know about… Pillow talk with lover boy?"

"Bielke was never my lover," Maggie said through clenched teeth.

"Oh no? Then why did I see him at your door? Your husband did too. The police were most interested."

"You told the police?"

"I felt it was my duty. And then, Bielke winds up dead. Victim of a jealous husband," said Trueblood-Fitch sanctimoniously.

Maggie had an intuitive flash.

"It was you. You killed Bielke. Because of the blackmail. If it became known you were a thief, you'd be finished. And you weren't only going to take some Raynham antiques. You'd gone out to try to find that snowdrop. To steal it. That's why you had a trowel."

"Yes. It's a great weapon. Bielke was so surprised when I slashed his throat. I guess none of his victims had ever fought back before. He knew he was done for. His blood spurting out. And then driving that trowel into his heart. His black heart. That was sweet. He thought he could blackmail me! Me! Lionel Trueblood-Fitch!"

The man was irate.

"And then you tried to blame it on Thomas."

"He'd made that easy enough. The police stopped looking at any other suspect as soon as they heard what I had to say."

"You'd let an innocent man go to prison?"

"Better him than me."

Then, without warning, Trueblood-Fitch pulled a small pistol from his pocket.

"And now the police can think one of those stupid Swedes killed you in revenge for what happened to Bielke."

He fired. There was a flash, intense pain, and Maggie dropped.

"Should I frame that idiot Anna Sofia? Or perhaps Constance…" he mused.

Trueblood-Fitch was taking more careful aim for a second shot, when he heard someone cry, "Noooooo."

He whirled around. Damien leapt at him and they went down and grappled. The gun went off again, harmlessly, into the air.

Derek hopped about, not sure what to do, until he saw a large bag of fertiliser lying against the greenhouse's foundation. He picked it up.

"Day, get out of the way."

Damien rolled to the side and Derek brought the bag down with all his strength on Trueblood-Fitch's head.

"Take that, home-wrecker," Derek shrieked.

The bag split open and covered the journalist with manure. He lay still.

Derek kicked away Trueblood-Fitch's pistol and Damien scrambled to his feet.

"Maggie?"

Maggie had collapsed face down on the ground. She held her side. A pool of blood was growing beneath her.

"Oh my God. Damien. Do something!" Derek was frantic.

"I'll call for an ambulance. And the police."

Damien pulled out his mobile.

Mrs Cook rushed up.

"I thought I heard shots."

She saw Maggie. "Oh dear Lord."

She bent and looked at the wound and shook her head. She took off her sweater and thrust it at Derek.

"Here. Hold this up against the wound. Try to stem the bleeding."

"Oh dear. I don't know if I…"

"Just do it," snapped Mrs Cook.

Trueblood-Fitch stirred. He moaned. Damien promptly sat down on him.

"Keep still or I'll hurt you again," Derek warned.

"I need to get towels and a blanket. Call for help. Hurry." Mrs Cook said.

Damien noticed the phone in his hand.

"Oh. I was going to do that."

Chapter 29

Sergeant Patrick came to tell Thomas all charges against him had been dropped and he was free to go.

"What? Why? What happened? Did you..."

"That's all I'm at liberty to say at this time. However, Mr Conyers is waiting for you. And... merry Christmas."

William thought his father looked exhausted. And old.

"The car's parked around the side," was all he said.

William was driving the Volvo estate that Gweneth usually used. After they had been driving a few minutes, Thomas noticed they had not taken the direction for Beaumatin.

"Where are we..."

"Our place. You can wash. Put on some fresh clothes. And we need to talk."

In fifteen minutes they had pulled up in front of William's home, a rambling house built at the turn of the last century on the outskirts of Cheltenham.

William took his father upstairs to a bedroom where some clean clothes were laid out on a bed.

"Fortunately we're more or less the same size. You know where the bathroom is," William pointed.

"Gweneth, James, Victoria and the children are visiting the Ainswicks. Come down to my study when you've changed."

When Thomas entered the study, he was surprised to find Derek Fiske and Damien Hawking there with William. He felt both relieved and disappointed not to see Maggie. He had been sure Maggie would have been there.

"Fiske? Hawking?"

William handed his father a tumbler of whisky and said, "You need to hear what these men have to say."

"Do I?" Thomas was frosty.

"Yes. You do. So sit down," said Damien firmly.

"Yes. It's Christmas. Don't you think we have other things we'd rather be doing? Only this is important," insisted Derek.

Thomas reluctantly sat.

Derek began, "Constance's wedding brought two very bad men to Beaumatin. The first was that Lionel Trueblood-Fitch. He'd talked Constance into letting him do the photography as well as an article on the wedding and the estate at Christmas, but he also saw it as an opportunity to nose around. Because our Lionel is a trifle light-fingered. Those things that went missing. Did you know some things were missing?"

Thomas shook his head.

"Oh. I guess no one wanted you to be bothered, given you were already in a snit. So Mrs Cook must have only told Maggie. Who told us. Anyhow, some things had disappeared. A snuff box from that display case in your library. A dagger from that cabinet with all those antique weapons. And those two ugly, ugly Staffordshire dogs you have in your drawing room. Mrs Cook was distraught and

Maggie figured that whoever had taken the things had to be someone who was there for the wedding.

"It turned out to be Trueblood-Fitch. We checked with some other places where he'd done stories. They'd also had some thefts. Some jewellery. Small antiques. Easily concealed in a suitcase or even a jacket pocket. And always when there were enough people around so that it would be hard to know who had taken them. And difficult to make any accusations."

Damien continued.

"The second bad man was Franz Bielke. Nils' uncle. His mother's brother. Bielke acted like he had money, but he didn't. He made ends meet by blackmailing people."

"Blackmail?"

"Yes. Nils' other uncle? His father's brother? Carl Magnus? His wife, Elisabeth? Bielke seduced her, then blackmailed her to keep him from telling Carl Magnus. She's given him close to £25,000 pounds."

"How did you find that out?"

Derek said, "Both Maggie and Damien could tell there had been something between poor Elisabeth and Bielke. Bielke made sure Elisabeth didn't get a chance to talk to Maggie, but didn't think about Damien. Damien's a good listener. And Elisabeth was concerned for Maggie."

"Indeed?"

"Oh don't be such a wanker, Raynham," Damien burst out.

Derek tittered.

"Sorry. But you need to hear what we have to say. Continue, Derek."

"Bielke decided to see if he could try the same thing with Maggie as he had with Elisabeth. Only Maggie wanted nothing to do with him, of course. And you should have known that," said Derek accusingly.

"That scene in the ballroom you walked in on? He came in and importuned her. Don't you just love that word? Importuned? She was trying to fight him off when you rushed up all cave man and thought you were breaking up some sort of tryst. And you wouldn't listen to Maggie when she tried to tell you what had actually happened. In fact, you'd refused to listen to her earlier when she came to ask you for help.

"Then the day of the wedding, in the afternoon? Bielke tried to get into Maggie's room. Except she was taking a shower and had locked the door. So he couldn't get in. Luckily. He was turning to walk away when you came along. He was happy to let you think he had just been coming out of Maggie's bedroom. And you fell for it. And apparently Trueblood-Fitch also saw you and Bielke outside of Maggie's room.

"The next morning, Bielke told Maggie what you'd seen and that he'd tell you what had really happened if she gave him £20,000.

"Maggie told him to go to hell."

"That's our Maggie," said Damien.

Thomas felt like a weight which had been almost too much to bear had suddenly been lifted. He realised what an idiot he'd been not to have listened to Maggie. And trusted her. And where was Maggie? Why wasn't she there?

"But then Bielke was murdered and everyone thought you had done it."

"Which you'd made pretty easy."

"Everyone but Maggie."

"And she convinced us and got us to promise to help find out who did, er, do it."

"The Three Musketeers."

"Minus D'Artagnan."

"Nils would make a cute D'Artagnan," Derek pointed out.

"Really, Derek."

"And Maggie tried to convince Inspector Willis that she was the one who had killed Bielke."

"She gave quite a persuasive performance. If she hadn't chosen a career in academia, she could have been a successful actress," added William.

"What? Why?"

"To give him a suspect besides yourself."

Thomas shook his head. Pig-headed...

"But Willis didn't believe her. Or he didn't want to."

Thomas thought about the close relationship the detective seemed to have with his wife. He scowled.

"So who did kill Bielke?" he finally asked.

"Trueblood-Fitch. Bielke had seen him take your snuff box and was trying to blackmail him as well. There was a confrontation and Trueblood-Fitch killed him. And then convinced the police it was you," said Damien.

"But why in the garden? And with a trowel?"

"No idea," said Damien.

"We're not the Shell answer man," Derek added.

Finally Thomas asked, "And where's Maggie? Tell me she didn't succeed in getting Willis to arrest her and that's why…"

"No. Willis has arrested Trueblood-Fitch," William said.

"But only after he shot Maggie," added Derek.

"What?" Thomas leapt up.

"Really, Derek. I'm sorry. He has an unfortunate penchant for the dramatic, does our Derek," said Damien apologetically.

"William…" A frantic Thomas turned to his son.

"Maggie is in Cheltenham General."

"Why didn't you tell me immediately?"

"Because it wasn't clear to me, or to any of us, in fact, whether you'd care," said William coolly.

"But of course I'd care."

"Really?"

Thomas flushed.

"How is she? Is she all right?"

"No, she's not all right. She was shot," Derek began, but William stopped him.

"Fortunately Trueblood-Fitch is not as good a shot as Maggie. The bullet went into her right side, just grazed a rib or two, and exited. Giles Sumner operated and repaired the damage. He says she should recover."

"But she lost a lot of blood before the ambulance arrived. You're lucky you have Mrs Cook," added Damien.

Thomas nodded.

"Take me to her."

William raised his eyebrows.

"Please, William."

William stood, followed by Derek and Damien.

Thomas gestured awkwardly. "And, er, thank you. All of you. I know I've acted like a complete ass. I'm sorry."

"It's Maggie you need to tell you're sorry," Derek said.

"I know."

Susan Alexander

Chapter 30

Maggie became aware that she was lying in a bed. Not a bed she knew, though. And there was someone in the room. Sitting by her bed. Who was it? Was it Thomas? She hoped it was Thomas, even though with the wish came the realisation that Thomas' presence was unlikely.

No. It was Inspector Willis.

"Maggie?"

She lifted a hand in a gesture of greeting.

"Merry Christmas."

Christmas? Was it Christmas? If so, it was the worst Christmas ever, Maggie decided.

"How are you?" Willis sounded concerned.

"Hard to say. Numb, at the moment."

Her voice was hoarse. Willis picked up a glass of water on a table by the bed and held a straw to her lips so she could sip.

"Thank you. That's better. But please. What happened?"

"You mean besides you getting shot by Trueblood-Fitch?"

Oh. Yes. She vaguely remembered Trueblood-Fitch. And the greenhouse. And a gun. But nothing much beyond that.

"Yes. Besides getting shot."

"Your friends, Fiske and Hawking, prevented him from firing again. They were surprisingly effective. Fortunately for you."

Maggie managed a faint smile.

"Your Mrs Cook also heard the shot. You're lucky she trained as a nurse, given how long it takes to get an ambulance out to that place of yours."

"It looks like I need to write a few thank you notes." Maggie tried to joke.

Willis wasn't smiling.

"You've arrested Trueblood-Fitch, then?"

"Yes."

"For Bielke's murder as well as…"

"Yes. We found a pair of shoes in his room. Once your housekeeper decided to be helpful and tell us where it was. The shoes still had some blood on their soles. And a butt from one of those fancy cigarettes Bielke smoked was stuck in the treads. And they matched some prints we found at the scene."

"Trueblood-Fitch didn't like wearing Wellies," Maggie said.

She wanted to ask if that meant Thomas had been released, but Willis was not volunteering that information.

"And asking under the circumstances would be the act of a lesser woman, and you are not a lesser woman," she told herself sternly.

Willis was watching her.

"Maggie, why in God's name did you try to make me think you had murdered Bielke?"

"Oh dear. I am sorry about that. But I knew Thomas hadn't killed Bielke. And I was fairly certain you thought that he had. Well, you arrested him. Despite my efforts."

Maggie paused and gestured for some more water.

"Thank you. Anyway, I had hoped that if you were suspicious of me, it would not only divert your attention away from Thomas as your chief suspect, but also encourage you to take a closer look at some of the others. I knew one of them had to be the murderer. It was just a question of discovering who. And I swear I didn't tell you anything that wasn't completely true."

"But how could you be so certain it wasn't Raynham?"

"How could you be so certain it wasn't me?" Maggie challenged.

Willis thought if he were a suspect, this would be where his solicitor would say, "My client is not going to answer that question."

"That's not the point. Raynham is. He's pathologically jealous. Possessive. Suspicious. And he's becoming increasingly violent. He punched Stephen Draycott. He knocked out one of Bielke's teeth. I saw the scratch on your neck from when he ripped off those pearls. And what was left of your ball dress. And I saw the preliminary report of what forensics found on it."

Maggie flushed and looked away.

"I had to find out what had happened. And if Bielke had attacked you. You refused to co-operate," he stated unapologetically.

"And these bruises…"

He reached over, lifted her arm and turned it. Faint purple marks still showed.

"That was Bielke."

"Bielke? So he did…"

"No. He tried, but I, er, discouraged him."

Willis thought about that but decided not to be diverted.

He continued. "Raynham even hit you. I know about the black eye."

Maggie didn't ask how he knew all these things. He was a detective. He detected.

"That was an accident."

"Yes. He was going for Einhorn."

Willis was irate.

"And don't forget. I saw him attack you. In his study."

"He wasn't attacking me. I'm clumsy. I tripped and took him down with me."

"Oh really?"

"Inspector Willis, I assure you, Thomas does not… abuse me."

"I see. Maybe it's just that you like it rough?"

Willis was feeling frustrated and lashed out. The words were spoken before he could stop himself.

Maggie had the stricken look of a deer caught in the headlights.

"Maggie. I'm sorry. I didn't mean…"

Something must have registered on the monitors to which Maggie was connected and two nurses rushed in. One glared at Willis while the other adjusted a setting on a box that was measuring some clear fluid that dripped into an IV tube.

Willis cursed himself. He had a fleeting moment of empathy with Raynham. What was it about this woman that would provoke him into saying such a thing?

One of the nurses—the glarer—said, "Five minutes. No more." They left.

Maggie was lying back with her eyes closed.

"Maggie?"

She opened her eyes. They were so green.

"Maggie, I'm sorry, I…"

Maggie raised her free hand and made a feeble gesture that from a cleric would have been a sign of blessing and forgiveness.

Willis took a deep breath.

"So what made you suspect Trueblood-Fitch?"

"Besides his being an odious toad? Well, some things had disappeared. Valuable things. An antique snuff box. A medieval dagger. Two porcelain figurines. Mrs Cook was completely distraught. Then Damien searched Trueblood-Fitch's room while Derek, er, distracted him.

"Did you know Trueblood-Fitch hit on Derek? With Damien looking on? He was a kind of gay version of Bielke. Anyway, Damien found the things he had taken. Hidden inside some socks in a drawer in his room. So we knew he was a bad guy even if we weren't sure he was the murderer.

"And then there was his interest in the snowdrop."

"Snowdrop?"

"I had noticed an unusual snowdrop. An early blooming one. Trueblood-Fitch was with me at the time so I pretended I hadn't, but the place where Bielke was murdered? It was the same place I had seen the snowdrop. Only I had gone back on my own and removed it. Potted it and put it someplace safe. But someone went back there after I had gone. With a trowel. And killed Bielke with it.

"And when Trueblood-Fitch shot me? It was because I found him trying to break into the greenhouse. I had locked it because there are some very valuable plants inside and with all the people around for the wedding. And the dogs having been sent to Ned's because of so many guests. Well, it just seemed to me that a preventative measure might be a good idea.

"Oh. And before he shot me, Trueblood-Fitch said that Bielke had noticed him taking the snuff box and was trying to blackmail him as well. Bielke approached him when he had gone back to look for that snowdrop. That was why Trueblood-Fitch killed him. In that place. With a trowel.

"Because Trueblood-Fitch had noticed what had been going on with Thomas and Bielke and me, he tried to put the blame on Thomas. Which was successful. Since you did arrest him."

"He's been released," Willis admitted reluctantly.

Maggie closed her eyes to hide the pain she felt. Thomas hadn't come. She had hoped he would come. So it was over.

"So Bielke was murdered because he was blackmailing Trueblood-Fitch for taking a snuff box while Trueblood-Fitch was trying to steal a snowdrop? It had nothing to do with you and…" Willis asked incredulously.

"So it would seem."

Willis shook his head. Then he said, "And what about your stepdaughter? Constance. She really hates you, you know. And was ready to swear in court that she'd seen you going into the garden with a trowel. And wearing Raynham's jacket."

"I know. And I'm sure she would have convinced herself that she was telling the truth."

"How did she find out about the trowel? We were careful not to say how Bielke was killed. In fact, when we questioned her previously, she assumed Bielke had been shot."

"I'm afraid I may have mentioned…"

"But why? Do you expect me to believe you didn't know what she would do with that information?"

"No. She did exactly what I thought she would do."

"Then…"

"It would have damaged any case you had against Thomas. If not wrecked it completely."

"But you might have been arrested..."

"I was aware of that risk. It seemed worth it."

Willis was dumbfounded. Could she possibly love Raynham so much that she was willing to face going to prison for him? What did she see in that snotty, po-faced prig who treated her so badly?

The nurse appeared in the doorway to indicate that Willis' time was up. The detective stood.

"Maggie, I…"

"You know. I can't keep on calling you Inspector Willis. At least when you're not officially interrogating me. Don't you have another name? Or are you like Inspector Morse, who was always just 'Morse.'"

Willis hesitated.

"What? Is it something awful? Like Hildegard? Aloysius? Engelbert? Carbuncle?"

Willis smiled reluctantly. Finally he said, "No. It's, er, Thomas."

"Thomas?"

"Yes. But my friends call me Tom. Or Tommy."

"Tom, then. If it's all right with you that I consider myself a friend?"

Willis wanted to tell her the other ways he would like her to consider him, but knew that would be madness. So he said, "Of course. And I'll be back to see you again tomorrow."

He added as an excuse, "As I am sure I will have some additional questions."

Susan Alexander

Chapter 31

Thomas found Willis coming out of Maggie's room. The detective looked grim.

Thomas put his hand on Willis' arm.

"How is she?"

Willis stared back at the other man and did not try to hide his contempt.

"You don't deserve her," he finally said and shrugged off Thomas' hand before he turned and walked away.

"I know," said Thomas softly to the back of the retreating policeman.

He went in and found Maggie with tubes going in and out. Bags hung from an IV stand and a couple of monitors registered numbers and wiggly lines beside her bed. She was surrounded by a garden of Christmas plants he assumed had come from Derek and Damien.

Maggie saw Thomas and thought he looked like a man who had been in a shipwreck and spent days adrift at sea. But then she decided it was the pain killers that were making her fanciful.

They stared at each other.

Finally Thomas said, "By all rights you should just tell me to get out."

Maggie thought about this.

"Do I have to?" she replied.

It took a moment for the meaning of her words to register.

Thomas grabbed her nearest hand and kissed the back and then turned it over and kissed the palm and then tears started running down his cheeks.

"Oh Thomas. Please don't cry. I want to hold you and I can't."

Thomas struggled to get himself under control.

After a while he managed to ask, "How are you?"

"I'm fine. I'm all right." Maggie paused. "Except for having been shot. Which is just as unpleasant as one would imagine it to be."

"Giles Sumner operated. I saw him on my way up here and he said the bullet went right through your side and managed to miss most of the important bits."

"Most. Yes. Lucky me."

Thomas sat down beside the bed. He still held her hand.

"My dear, I'm so sorry. So very, very sorry. I acted like an idiot. Again."

"Yes, you did. And you refused to listen to me when I needed your help and tried to tell you about Bielke. And you jumped to a wrong conclusion. Again. I thought you were going to try not to do that."

Thomas knew there was nothing he could say in his defence, so he asked, "Is there anything I can do?"

Maggie looked at him thoughtfully. Finally she said, "Yes."

"What? Anything. Just tell me. I'll do…"

"I know the plan was for the wedding festivities at Beaumatin to continue through New Year's. But given all that's happened. Is there any way people could just… go home?"

"Go home?"

"Yes. I don't mean Mrs Cook and Ned and Jamie and Ian and Wesley of course. But could the Swedes go back to Sweden? And the Genevans back to Geneva? And the Londoners to London? And everyone else back to wherever he came from? I gather Willis has already removed Trueblood-Fitch and I suspect that ferrety Knowles has fled. But all the others?"

Thomas leaned over and kissed Maggie on the forehead.

"Mon pauvre papillon. Of course I can send people home. In fact, the more I consider it, I more I think it's an excellent idea."

"Thank you. Giles said if everything stays all right I should be out of here by New Year's Eve day and can go home to finish recuperating. Strange…" Maggie's voice trailed off.

"What's strange, my dear?"

But Maggie had fallen asleep.

Susan Alexander

Chapter 32

The next morning, Maggie was surprised to see William stroll into her room. Normally visiting hours did not begin until the late afternoon. Unless they had been changed because it was Boxing Day. Or because he was here as her legal representative. Or perhaps he had invoked the 28th Baron Raynham. Or would it be the 29th? However he had managed it, Maggie decided she didn't care and was just glad to see him.

William looked at Maggie, with all her tubes and bags and monitors.

"Are you all right?" he asked, concerned.

Maggie tried to smile. "I'm fine. Or at least as well as can be expected."

"Happy Boxing Day. And a belated merry Christmas," he said, trying to sound jovial.

"Thank you. The same to you. In fact, I got some gifts for the children…"

"That is very kind. But don't worry. The children are quite happy with what Santa brought them."

He paused.

"You saw my father?"

"Yes. He was… repentant."

"You know. The way he treated you. No one would blame you… I certainly wouldn't…"

Maggie held up her hand.

"William. It was a perfect storm. Hordes of von Fersens. Bielke. Trueblood-Fitch. Knowles. All those fairy lights. The miracle is that he didn't murder Bielke. Or that I didn't. Had I been able to get to the gun room at the right moment I'm sure I would have shot him with a clear conscience. He was a horrible person.

"And I still…"

She stopped. She was not going to discuss her feelings for Thomas with his son. Not when she didn't even discuss her feelings for Thomas with the man himself.

William finished Maggie's sentence on his own. He changed the subject.

"I spoke with Ulrika von Fersen. And Georg Axel. I told them everything the way it really happened and am letting them tell the others. In Swedish. So there will be no misunderstandings."

"Including about Elisabeth?" Maggie was concerned.

"No. That didn't seem necessary."

"That's good. And thank you."

"And I corrected any wrong impressions about you that they might have gotten from my unsatisfactory sister."

"Oh."

"My father had a talk with her."

"Oh?"

"She wasn't very… Well, I can only hope that at some point she will grow up."

"Nils is a good man."

"I hope he is a patient one."

William looked at Maggie.

"I can see that you're tired. But there is someone here who would like to see you."

"All right." Maggie was curious.

William went out and, to Maggie's surprise, returned with Ulrika von Fersen.

"I'll wait outside," he said and left the two women together.

The matriarch regarded Maggie critically.

"How are you?"

"I'm all right, thank you. Recovering."

"I see."

There was a pause.

"I came because I wanted to apologize. For my family. They took advantage of you. And were not properly appreciative. We should have known that Constance… Well, it should have occurred to me at least that her offer of hospitality was not entirely straightforward.

"And also for introducing that Franz Bielke into your home. We all knew what he was. And my foolish daughters-in-law. Foolish each in her own way…"

She looked closely at Maggie.

"Ah. I see you know about Elisabeth. She can live with her guilty conscience. As for Carl Magnus. Best he remain ignorant. I am sure you agree."

Maggie nodded.

"And as for Anna Sofia. If she wishes to make her brother a martyr, that is Georg Axel's problem. As far as I'm concerned she can remember the man any way she likes, now that he is dead and can do no more harm.

"I understand you will be here for the rest of the week at least. So we will all be gone before you come home. But I wanted to say, if you are ever in Stockholm, to let me know. I would enjoy returning your hospitality and having some conversations with you. You seem like an intelligent and sensible woman. It is a pity there are so few of us."

Ulrika patted Maggie's hand. She rose and walked out, ramrod straight, supported by her cane.

Maggie was just on the brink of sleep when she had another visitor. It was Inspector Willis.

He looked at her flushed cheeks and bright eyes and felt her forehead. He scowled.

"You have a fever."

"Yes. It's normal. They're giving me…"

"I'll be right back."

Willis left. Maggie heard voices in the hall. He returned.

"Someone will be in to check on you shortly."

He sat down beside the bed.

"I thought you'd like to know. Trueblood-Fitch is cooperating. He's confessed to killing Bielke. As for shooting you, Fiske and Hawking witnessed him do it, so there's not much he can say. Especially with the supporting forensic evidence. His gun, the bullets we recovered, GSR on his hand and jacket. He'll probably spend the rest of his life in prison."

Maggie felt a twinge of… what. Pity? The man was a thief. He had brutally murdered another man. He would have killed her if Derek and Damien had not intervened. So why should she feel more sorry for him than for his victim?

"No more loud tweed," she said.

Willis looked puzzled.

"Oh. There is one thing," Maggie said.

"Yes?"

"Bielke was also blackmailing Elisabeth von Fersen. Apparently she was more receptive to his advances than I was. Anyway. I understand there are pictures. And I wondered. Hoped. Well, that if you find them, that you could… destroy them. Since they have nothing at all to do with Bielke's murder."

Willis regarded Maggie.

"I won't even ask how you know all this. And neglected to mention it to me before now. In fact, we did find some pictures. Although I can't promise to destroy them. However, since, as you say, they have nothing to do with Bielke's murder, and Trueblood-Fitch has confessed, I see no reason for them to become public."

Maggie was relieved.

"Thank you. Franz Bielke was a bad man."

A nurse came in. Willis stood.

"I'll let you rest. I just wanted to give you an update. And I know where to find you if we have any further questions."

He patted her hand, hesitated, as though he wanted to say something more, then left.

The nurse checked Maggie's temperature. Went out and returned with another bag filled with clear liquid that she hung on the stand and connected to the IV.

"You need to rest," she said severely, as if Maggie had had anything to do with her stream of visitors.

Maggie closed her eyes and was just dropping off to sleep again when she sensed someone else had come into the room. She was debating whether to reveal that she was awake, when the person leaned over and kissed her forehead. She smelled whiffs of citrus and spice. It was Thomas.

She opened her eyes.

"Oh. Hi."

He frowned and felt her forehead.

"You have a fever."

"I know. The nurse was just in. She…"

Thomas left before she could finish her sentence.

Maggie heard voices in the hall. Thomas returned.

"The nurse said some policeman already told her you had a fever and she'd given you something. What policeman? Was it Willis?"

"Yes."

"What did he want?"

"To tell me that Trueblood-Fitch has confessed to murdering Bielke."

"That was his excuse for coming to see you?"

Maggie closed her eyes for a long moment. Then she opened them and asked, "Thomas? How are you?"

"Me? How am I?"

"Yes. You."

"I'm... fine."

"Really?"

"Well, the house is still full of Swedes. Apparently re-booking flights during the holidays is harder than you'd think. Even if you're a von Fersen.

"And I talked to Constance. It was not pleasant. She refuses to see... well, that she might have been partly responsible..."

Thomas decided he would not mention Constance's conviction that everything that had gone wrong was all Maggie's fault and her wish that Trueblood-Fitch had taken his second shot at Maggie.

"And there are still fairy lights everywhere you look and... I miss you."

"Me too. I mean..."

Thomas kissed her. Sighed.

"I'm so sorry, Papillon. You look completely done in. So sleep. I'll be right here."

He settled in the chair beside her bed and pulled out an *Economist*.

Maggie slept for an hour, then was woken by an aide coming in with lunch. Thomas was still sitting next to her bed.

Maggie looked at the contents of the tray, then pushed it away.

"I'd rather eat potted shrimp."

Maggie was not at all fond of the classic British dish.

"You have to eat," said Thomas sternly.

"I'd need Viognier to wash it down."

"You can't…"

"I know, I know."

"If you're going to be pig-headed, I'll just have to go out and get you something."

Maggie looked under the metal cover at her lunch again.

"I am not pig-headed. Would you eat this?" she indicated what was on the plate.

Thomas' mouth twitched. But he stood.

"Very well."

"Oh Thomas. Please. No. You don't have to… I'm really not at all hungry."

"You have to eat," he repeated and left.

Maggie pushed the stand away that held her tray and tried to fall back to sleep. Before she could, someone else came into the room. It was Elisabeth von Fersen.

"Elisabeth."

"I wanted to see how you were," said the woman.

Maggie gestured at the tubes and the bags and the monitors.

"And to say…"

"You did try to warn me."

"Yes. But then Franz said if I told you. About the blackmail. That he'd tell Carl Magnus about us."

"Oh. You should know. The police found the pictures."

"Oh no." Elisabeth looked panicked.

"No. No, it's all right. I spoke with Inspector Willis. And he said you don't have to worry. They are not going to show them in court. Or to anyone else."

"Really?" Elisabeth slumped in relief. Her eyes filled with tears.

"I've been so scared," she sniffed.

"I'd been married thirty years. Carl Magnus is a good husband. But predictable. And I was getting older and had begun to ask myself, 'Is this all there is?' Franz noticed.

"He speaks perfect French. I mean he spoke perfect French. He would recite Baudelaire. And Rimbaud. And Verlaine. It was so romantic. He was everything Carl Magnus was not. I knew he was a bad man. Dangerous. But somehow that just added to the attraction. Until I found out just how bad. Can you understand?"

Maggie nodded.

"I watched him pursuing you. I knew he was causing you to have problems with your husband. But I was too afraid to speak out. I fear I lack your… courage."

"It's all right, Elisabeth. And it's over. You needn't be afraid any longer."

"I can hardly believe it. It's been so long since…"

"I can imagine."

"Anyway. I wanted to say I am sorry. That I didn't speak out. And to say I hope you are well soon. And to give you this."

Elisabeth reached into her purse and handed Maggie a small jeweller's box.

"Oh, Elisabeth. No."

"Please. Open it and I will tell you."

Maggie opened the box. Inside was a ring. It was a large ice blue stone surrounded by what Maggie assumed were diamonds in an elaborate, art-deco mounting.

"Franz gave it to me. When we were first… He said he wanted me to wear it to remind me of him. When we were at family dinners, parties, events. He liked seeing me wear it when I was with Carl Magnus. The colour of the stone matched his eyes.

"When Carl Magnus asked me about it, I said it had been my mother's. It's a blue diamond. I had it checked.

When... when the blackmail began. I think he received it from another of his victims."

"That's quite possible. When he asked me to pay him so he would tell Thomas we were *not* having an affair as he had made Thomas believe, he said I could always give him the diamonds from the Raynham family jewels. That he had a friend who could make fake copies."

From Elisabeth's shocked expression, Maggie guessed William had not included Bielke's attempt to blackmail her in his narrative to the von Fersens of what had happened.

"I told him I wouldn't. Pay him. And then just a couple of hours later, he was killed by Trueblood-Fitch, whom he was also trying to blackmail."

Elisabeth nodded.

"But Elisabeth, I can't accept this."

"Please. Take it. For me it will be my celebration of freedom from that awful man. And for you. Think of it as, as a victory trophy. Like, what did your native Indians used to do? Like a scalp. A symbol of your triumph. Over a very bad man. Two very bad men."

Maggie repressed a shudder, but said, "If you insist."

"I do," said Elisabeth.

Her left brain added, "And it will be useful the next time Thomas forbids us to wear the Raynham jewels."

Her right brain responded, "Although light blue isn't really one of our colours."

Maggie looked around. "But I can't keep it here. I don't even have a purse."

"I'll give it to your housekeeper. Mrs Cook? And ask her to put it someplace safe until you are back home."

Maggie knew when she was defeated.

"And now I should go and let you rest. You look tired. I guess that's not surprising."

Maggie was exhausted, but found that when she tried to doze off, she couldn't. She thought about Bielke. And how someone who had such ability and was so privileged could have become so terrible. Although in the end he had suffered the consequences of his actions. Was that justice? At least Elisabeth was free of the man.

And what about herself and Thomas? And the damage Bielke had caused. Thomas was in his "I'm so sorry, I've been an idiot" mode. Which would last until… The next time? Would Thomas change? Maggie had her doubts. As for herself, she wasn't sure she had many "next times" left in her.

Then she decided her thoughts were being affected by being shot and the fever and the medications and the whole being-in-the-hospital thing. And that she should probably not think about much of anything until she was feeling better.

"Denial!" shouted her left brain.

"Later!" said her right.

More visitors. This time it was Lady Ainswick and Anne Brooks. Anne was her usual perky self and was wearing a Christmas jumper featuring a reindeer with a large red nose.

"One of the boys gave it to me. He thought it was funny," she explained.

"I thought you were in Devon," Maggie said to Anne.

"Gweneth told me you'd been shot. I called Anne and here we are," explained Beatrix.

"We'd just gotten back this morning. And it seems like you've had another adventure," Anne remarked.

Maggie nodded.

"Although I suspect this was all a ploy on your part to get away from your houseguests. And Constance," said Anne shrewdly.

"Not guilty. If I'd really felt compelled to flee, I would have found a way that was slightly less… dramatic," Maggie replied.

"And I would have chosen someplace much more pleasant," she added,

"Did Constance really invite ten members of Nil's family to stay at Beaumatin? Plus herself and Nils? And for two whole weeks? Aren't there some nice hotels nearby?" Anne was indignant.

"Sixteen days, in fact. Although now there are only nine von Fersens. And I believe they have decided to shorten their stay. Under the circumstances."

"I should hope so," agreed Anne.

"That girl," said Beatrix.

Before anything further could be said, two more visitors entered. It was Celia Sumner and Lady Nesbitt. Celia was a sporty blonde in her forties. Thalia was two decades older, heavyset and had steel-grey hair cut short. But Maggie knew that under her formidable exterior the woman was kind and caring. Both were members of the local Church Ladies' Guild. Thomas' wife Harriet had been an active participant and Maggie had felt that some involvement on her part was expected.

"Maggie! Giles told me what happened. I'm so sorry," said Celia, who was the wife of Maggie's surgeon.

"And of course, Celia told me," explained Thalia.

Thalia and Beatrix eyed each other. Relations between the two had never been particularly warm. Maggie knew it was an issue of incompatible personalities rather than anything specific.

"What an awful way to spend the holidays," sympathised Celia.

"Although after the wedding and the ball, you are probably enjoying the rest. And the peace and quiet," Thalia commented.

Maggie was tempted to reply she was getting little of either but stopped herself. People were only being kind.

The ladies chatted about their Christmas celebrations and their families until Anne looked at Maggie and said, "Well, I am glad you seem to be doing well, but you doubtless need to get some rest."

Everyone agreed and promised they would return to see her again soon. Maggie sighed when they left.

Wolcum Yole

However, they had only been gone a minute when Thomas returned, carrying a large shopping bag. He took the tray off the stand and put it on the floor by the door. Then from the bag he took a prettily embroidered place mat and matching napkin, a china soup bowl and a silver soup spoon. He arranged them on the stand.

Next he pulled out a crystal goblet and a bottle of Maggie's favourite mineral water.

"I know it's not Viognier. Or Meursault. But it will have to do," he said as he filled the glass.

He removed a thermos and poured Mrs Cook's famous butternut squash soup into the bowl. It steamed.

"Mrs Cook says to tell you how sorry she is she couldn't come in person, but she doesn't feel she can leave with the house full of von Fersens. However, she's promised to send soup and anything else you'd like until you're out of here."

"Coffee?" Maggie asked hopefully.

"Only if Giles says it's all right," replied Thomas firmly.

"Now eat!" he commanded. "I need you to get better and come home."

SUSAN ALEXANDER

Chapter 33

As Giles Sumner had promised, on New Year's Eve day, Thomas drove Maggie back to Beaumatin as carefully as he could on the single track lane. She found the house still bedecked but deserted. Even Mrs Cook had gone to spend New Year's with her son and his family in Brighton.

Maggie stood in the grand hall and considered all the decorations.

"I know it's beautifully done, but it does seem a bit like gilding the lily."

"I agree. And I haven't even received the final invoice from Fiske and Hawking yet."

"And everyone's gone?"

"Yes."

"Constance and Nils?"

"Are enjoying a honeymoon in the Seychelles that I was able to arrange. They were both happy to trade in the rain for some sun."

Loki and Freya came out to greet her. Maggie was welcomed back in their low key, Tibetan mastiff way. Loki sniffed her, intrigued by the hospital smells. Freya let herself be hugged.

"Hi you guys. Where were you when I needed you? Yes, I know that's not fair. You would have been there, but you weren't allowed."

Maggie went into her study and collapsed on the sofa.

"Oof."

"Are you all right?" Thomas asked anxiously.

"I'm fine. Just… unaccustomed to being up and about. As a result of having been lying around too much recently." Maggie tried to joke.

Thomas looked sceptical.

After some chicken soup, left by Mrs Cook and reheated by Thomas, Maggie stood at the foot of the grand staircase and looked up.

"Let me carry you," Thomas offered.

"No. Thank you. It will be better if I do it myself. I don't expect to retain much dignity, though."

Supporting herself on the bannister, Maggie slowly made it up to the landing, then across, then up the second set of stairs to the floor above.

"Made it," she called down.

Thomas bounded up.

"You should lie down."

"I will. But first I want to shower. My personal hygiene has sunk to medieval levels. Why does that always seem to happen in a hospital? You'd think they'd try to have the opposite be the case."

"Saving on water and heating?" Thomas suggested.

Maggie went to her room. Looked around. Sighed.

There was a large jeweller's box on the bed. Tied with green ribbon. There was a card. It read, "Forgive me."

Wolcum Yole

Maggie opened the box and found the Raynham pearls, restrung, with a new clasp. It was an emerald. Edged in diamonds. She shook her head.

She took a long shower with a plastic bag inelegantly taped over her stitches. Then she slept through the afternoon.

Thomas had set up a table in the TV room to save Maggie from negotiating the stairs. As midnight approached, he excused himself, then returned with a pair of champagne flutes and a bottle of Krug.

"We seem to have quite a few of these. And Giles said it would be all right if you had one glass. One," he stressed.

"Strange New Year's Eve. Usually I'm at some faculty party. What do you normally do?" she asked.

"It depends. We'd go to William's or William and Gweneth would come here or we'd all go to the Ainswicks. Although in recent years I must admit I've tended more towards cursing the darkness than lighting candles."

Thomas popped the champagne cork and filled two glasses.

"Um, Thomas?"

Thomas paused. "Yes?"

Maggie took a deep breath. She needed to say something she didn't want to say and was feeling sick to her stomach with anxiety. But she was not a lesser woman and only a lesser woman would shirk from saying something that needed to be said.

"Thomas, I know you told me in the past that you find me, um, elusive. Which you say has led to some…

misunderstandings. And issues with trust. And I know I've never said... Well, because I didn't think it needed to be said. But perhaps it does. Although surely you must know that... that I... um, how very much I love you. And how you could think I would ever, um, desire someone else, or encourage someone, or that you'd believe I might have those sorts of feelings for someone besides you when I... I..."

Maggie stood up. Too suddenly. She clutched her side.

"I'm sorry. I find this all rather difficult."

She walked out and left Thomas holding the two glasses.

Thomas gave her five minutes. He drank a glass of champagne and then he went to find his wife.

Maggie had not gone far. She was in her room and from her puffy eyes and red nose Thomas gathered she had been crying.

He held her. "My poor dear. You must know how much I love you as well. To the point it makes me quite crazy at times. So crazy that I behave very badly and do things which I must later ask you to forgive. Fortunately for me, you seem to have an extraordinary capacity for forgiveness. Nevertheless, since it's New Year's, I want you to know that I have made a resolution to..."

"No. Don't tell me."

Thomas was surprised.

"In the Eliot family, everyone was supposed to make a resolution each year, but no one was supposed to tell any of the others what it was. I was told it was like making a birthday wish when you blow out the candles on your cake, but I think it was really because everyone was so competitive, people would have sabotaged each other's good intentions," she added thoughtfully.

"Of course, if your resolution included 'No more baubles...'"

"All the barons give their wives baubles. It's a Raynham tradition."

Maggie sighed, then said, "Oh. Speaking of Raynham traditions. I nearly forgot. Let me show you."

Maggie went into her dressing room. A moment later she emerged with a pot holding a quartet of snowdrops. Their long, gracefully curved white outer segments were lightly crinkled and streaked with pinstripes of pale green.

"I saw this in the far garden that has the early snowdrops. That dreadful Lionel Trueblood-Fitch was with me and seemed unusually interested, so I tried to pretend it was nothing special and sneaked back later and dug it up and potted it. And hid it. Since Loki and Freya were at Ned's and not on patrol. I think that's what Trueblood-Fitch was looking for when he killed Bielke. And shot me. For a society reporter, he seemed strangely interested in snowdrops."

Maggie handed Thomas the pot.

"Ah. That is where some insider knowledge about the galanthophile set is useful. Trueblood-Fitch has an aunt, Freda Fitch Wallace, who has a famous snowdrop garden in Herefordshire. She must be in her eighties and has no children of her own, only some nieces and nephews. Including Trueblood-Fitch. She is said to change her will frequently, depending on who is currently most in her favour. I suspect Trueblood-Fitch thought presenting her with a rare snowdrop would help his chances.

"And unless I'm mistaken, and I don't think I am, it is indeed a new snowdrop you have found." Thomas finished his examination.

"Really?"

"Yes. You have a good eye."

"Oh."

"And Beatrix tells me that greens are all the current rage."

"Green is the new yellow?"

Thomas looked confused.

Maggie laughed. "Never mind. I call it Wolcom Yole. After the poem used in Benjamin Britten's *A Ceremony of Carols*. Do you know it? It means welcome Yule, or welcome Christmas, in Middle English."

Maggie noticed Thomas' mouth twitch.

"Is it too obscure? Too academic? I'm sure you can come up with a better name..." she added.

"No. The person who finds a new snowdrop generally gets to name it. Wolcom Yole is fine. You are an Oxford don, after all. And if someone can't figure out what it means, he can always google it."

Thomas sat down in one of the chairs and pulled Maggie onto his lap. He put his arms around her and held her close.

"Ouch." She winced.

"I'm so sorry. Are you all right?"

"I'm fine. Or I will be. Although I'm not sure how I'll manage the book launch next week."

"Oh. The book launch. That's been postponed. Until at least the end of January."

"It has?"

Thomas was avoiding eye contact.

"Um. Yes. I contacted your Malcolm Fortescue-Smythe and explained that you'd had an accident and needed to recuperate. He's quite a fine fellow, by the way."

Being quite a fine fellow was Thomas' ultimate compliment, Maggie knew.

"You did your twenty-eighth baron routine," said Maggie accusingly.

"I didn't need to. He already knew."

Maggie sighed.

"Yes. Until Constance's wedding. I really had no idea I had married such an, um, socially prominent person."

"The twenty-seven previous barons we have on the walls didn't give you some idea?"

"Sorry. Oblivious. Blame it on my being American. And your being quite the recluse."

She thought. "But the end of January. That's Hilary term. How can I…"

"Um…"

"Yes?" Suspicious.

"I contacted Einhorn. And Carrington. They agreed you could be on leave until Trinity term and start being the Weingarten fellow then."

"That's not until late April," Maggie protested.

"My dear, I want you to be able to really recuperate. Giles says that will take a good month to six weeks. Longer if you overdo it, which would be like you. If you went back to work too soon."

Maggie glared.

"And I thought it would be nice for us to have some time together as well to, er, recuperate."

"Oh."

He held her closer.

"And it will be snowdrop season. Last year you were only here for, what, an hour or so? This way you can enjoy the full show. And you seem to have a surprising knack for them. For a social scientist."

Thomas glanced at his watch and sighed.

"It's after midnight. We have missed New Year's. And the champagne is probably less than chilled and lacking in bubbles at this point. I am turning you into as sad a case as myself. But I promise to do better next year."

"Next year?"

Maggie still had problems with the concept of relational long-termism. Thomas knew this. And even acknowledged much of it was his own fault.

"Yes, Papillon. Next year," he said firmly. "But meanwhile, it's time for bed."

Maggie had no problem with that at all.

Susan Alexander

G. elwesii Wolcom Yole

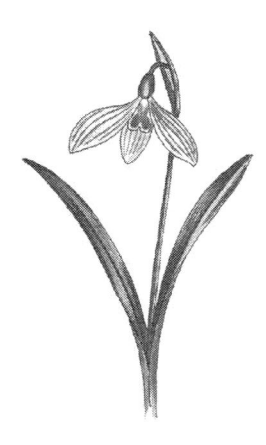

G. elwesii Wolcom Yole is an early blooming snowdrop. Short and upright, Wolcom Yole's symmetrical flowers are triangular in outline and dangle from a short pedicel. Long outer segments are textured and generously striped with green. Inner segments are marked in a lighter green hour-glass shape. Leaves are erect and olive green.

The snowdrop was first noticed in 2012 in the gardens of Beaumatin, Gloucestershire, by Lady Margaret Raynham. Because it blooms at Christmastime it was named "Wolcom Yole," after the Middle English poem used by Benjamin Britten in *A Ceremony of Carols*.

Susan Alexander

About the author

A native New Yorker, Susan Alexander lives in Luxembourg, where she writes and undertakes research on public policy and the social sciences.

She enjoys writing about women who have led complex and interesting lives, their relationships and the choices they have made. It frequently happens that there is some murder and mayhem involved in as well.

Made in the USA
Charleston, SC
04 February 2015